WASHED UP (WITH A KRAKEN)

TRAPPED WITH A MONSTER BOOK 2

L.E. ELDRIDGE

This book is a work of fiction. Names, characters, places, and incidents are the product of the author's imagination or are used fictitiously. Any resemblance to actual events, locales, or persons, living or dead, is coincidental.

Copyright © 2023 by L.E. Eldridge

All rights reserved.

No part of this book may be reproduced in any form or by any electronic or mechanical means, including information storage and retrieval systems, without written permission from the author, except for the use of brief quotations in a book review.

Cover Art: Bloodwrit

Cover Formatting: Clover Lane Designs

Copy editing and proofreading: Alexa Thomas at the Fiction Fix

Sensitivity read: Emeric Davis from Queerly Beloved Serivces

*To anyone who feels they can't be loved.
You can, and are.*

TRIGGER WARNINGS

This book contains:
 Intoxication, misogyny, foster care, nepotism, kidnapping, mentions of death, stockholm mentions, light mentions of D/s themes, sexually explicit scenes.

Enjoy ;)

PROLOGUE
QUINN

"Remember class, when in doubt, make sure you're not cutting through the meat. If you are, you're doing it wrong." Quinn set her butcher's knife on the bench and walked to the back sinks to wash her hands. The butchery unit wasn't her favorite, but it did give her a much greater respect for the meat she used.

As she put her apron away and got packed up, she turned to see Chef Tramis approaching her. Chef Tramis was one of the top in her field, and she was killer with a knife. She came to the Culinary Institute of America to do workshops often, and Quinn always signed up. This class, they focused on breaking down an entire cow. By the end, Quinn had worked up a serious sweat.

"Great job today, Quinn. You always try your best, and I like that about you."

Quinn was gushing inside, but she tried her hardest to keep a calm, cool demeanor. "Thank you, Chef. Your workshops are always so informative."

Chef Tramis smiled. "Thank you. Now tell me, how did the interview with Coastal Cruises go?"

"Amazing! I was interviewed by Chef Westly, and it seemed to go well."

Coastal Cruise Lines was one of the top externships at the Institute. It wasn't like a regular cruise: it was a summer long excursion to Hawaii, Singapore, Australia, Japan, and so many others. The cruise line set up workshops for hospitality and culinary students, where they could rub elbows with some of the top chefs in the industry. Plus, at the end, one or two got offered full-time positions. Not only did you get to travel for entire summers, but they paid so well, there was no real reason to work the rest of the year, even though Quinn probably would. That way, she could focus on working for herself as a private chef or caterer, so she wouldn't have to worry about working for the money.

Almost every student at the Institute applied, but only twenty or so got interviews. Out of those twenty, the cruise line only chose four or five. Quinn was confident in her abilities, and she had worked so hard to maintain a perfect 4.0 GPA on top of taking every extra workshop she could. She even picked up extra shifts at the on-campus restaurants, just to experience every side.

"Ah, yes," Chef Tramis continued. "Chef Westly is a colleague of mine. Maybe I can reach out and put in a good word for you."

Quinn's eyes widened. "Really? That would be amazing."

"Consider it done. You're a hard worker Quinn, and we need more of that in this industry."

She thanked her, and just as Quinn turned to leave, she ran headfirst into her arch nemesis. Yes, that may sound dramatic, but it was true. Brandon Cotley was an arrogant ass with a world-renowned chef as a father; he hadn't worked a hard day in his life. He skated by on his father's name and just assumed everything would be handed to him.

"Oh, sorry. I guess you couldn't see me with your head shoved so far up Chef's ass."

Quinn rolled her eyes, ignoring his comment, and walked around him. Over the years, she'd learned it was better to just walk away. Feeding into it only fueled the fire. To her great chagrin, he followed her out of the classroom and down the hall anyway.

"So, now that you have Tramis vouching for you, you may actually have a shot. I guess I'll be seeing you a lot this summer. My father donated a few new convection ovens to the kitchen, so there's no way I'm not going."

"Of course," Quinn said. "It's not like there's any other way you would have gotten in."

His face soured at that, and Quinn couldn't help but smirk. Since he never put in any real effort, comparing him to his father always worked.

To Quinn's delight, Brandon took the bait. "I could do it without him, but why not use the resources you're gifted with?"

Was he kidding? Even though she knew the answer was no, it was hard to think anyone was that unaware, especially anyone around sharp objects as frequently as he was. Quinn rolled her eyes but kept walking, hoping he'd get the message.

He, unfortunately, did not and cut her off, stepping in front of her and planting his arm against the wall, blocking her in. "So, since we'll be seeing each other a lot this summer, maybe we can see each other for other things." He grabbed a piece of her hair, twisting it around his fingers.

Quinn smacked his hand away and took a step back. "I

think not. I'll be spending my time learning and absorbing. Any time I do have off definitely won't be spent with you."

Brandon huffed and stepped back. "Whatever. You're not even that hot. You should stop sampling so much of your own food." With that, he left. *Thank god.* Men like Brandon would never understand that a woman's entire ego didn't start, or end, with their opinions.

Quinn shook off the interaction and made her way back to her dorm. She'd gotten lucky–her roommate for the semester never showed, so she had the entire dorm to herself. It was the first time in her life she'd had her own space. She grew up in the foster system, where she always had to share with at least one other person. The woman who ran the home she was placed in wasn't mean or unkind, just uninterested. There were a lot of other kids, and Quinn was a recluse anyway, so it never bothered her. When she got older, she started assisting with preparing meals. While the menus were always limited, it was her favorite part of the day.

Once she was old enough to work, she bussed tables at a nearby restaurant. She moved up quickly, eventually becoming a prep cook in the kitchen. The owner, Chef Deen, taught her proper knife cuts and different cooking techniques. Though it was just a diner, Chef Deen was talented, and she thanked her lucky stars for getting out of bussing tables.

She worked hard until she was able to apply to the Institute and leave. Chef Dean celebrated her success with a miniature cake, which was the only congratulations she ever received, and then she headed off. She was almost done with her education, and as soon as she got the Coastal Cruises internship, she would get the job and finally get to travel, cook, and do everything she's ever wanted to.

1

QUINN

Quinn pulled her small suitcase behind her, dragging it over the metal grate onto the ship. Her first, and hopefully only, plane ride had been quite the experience. She had been so worked up after her flight that she stayed up all night studying her notes. As soon as she could, she got out of that motel and hustled over to the ship, excited to finally get going.

The ship was giant–it had to be at least twelve decks. She wasn't even sure how this thing was floating; it looked like an entire city. Stepping onto the main deck, she noted it was extremely empty. She could see a large pool over to the left, and a bunch of loungers across the space, and a single fold up table to the right, a man sitting behind it on his phone.

He looked up with a quirked eyebrow as she joined him. "Hey, you a new employee?"

She nodded. "Kind of. I'm one of the culinary students."

"Perfect," he said, gathering some documents from the table. "Here's an employee handbook and some paperwork you'll have to fill out and give to the head chef before we set off. Galley check-in is on the third deck, to the right after you get off the elevator over there. Welcome aboard."

She took all her belongings and headed down. When the elevator opened, she was no longer in a place with wooden floors and bright colors. Instead, she was staring down a small white hallway with a bunch of corridors shooting off from it. With a deep breath, she made her way down the hall until she found an industrial kitchen. Everything was stainless steel, and built like a maze. Quinn drooled over all the giant mixers and other appliances. She grimaced when she saw the convection ovens that looked extra shiny and never used, reminding her of Brandon's impending presence.

"Hello," she heard a voice call deeper into the kitchen. She moved through the maze to find a woman with dark hair and a strong face, already dressed in chef whites.

"Hello," she said, her voice laced with a thick French accent. "I'm Chef Moreau, the sous chef here in the main galley. This galley preps most of the meals for the ship, but there are small restaurants and cafes scattered across the ship that you will spend time working in as well. The better you do, the better job you will be positioned for. It doesn't matter how high your class rank is or who you know. Here, it's about how you perform. Is that clear?"

"Yes, Chef," Quinn said, almost militarily.

"Good." She turned to move through the kitchen, and Quinn assumed she was supposed to follow. When they stopped at a pile of manila envelopes, she whirled around to face Quinn again. "What's your name?"

"Quinn Piker."

She perused them until she found one with her name on it. "Okay, Quinn, please have this filled out in the next few days. We have about a week until we board and set off. In that week, you will attend seminars covering everything you'll need to know while you're here, basics like kitchen safety and interacting with guests. There is an itinerary in the packet; your room number and key are in there as well. The staff rooms are on the floor below. Your orientation seminar starts at three, but you can go to your room and get unpacked until then."

"Yes, Chef. Thank you."

Chef Moreau nodded and Quinn found her way back through the maze to the elevator, eventually making it to the staff quarters. The halls were much tighter than upstairs, only fitting one person at a time. The key to her room had to be jiggled in the lock, but once she got it, she was actually surprised by the size of it. It was about the size of her dorm room back home, with two closets and a separate door she assumed was the bathroom. Honestly, she was relieved; she'd done some research, and some cruise ships had glorified closets for staff rooms.

She set to work putting all her belongings away and claimed the bottom bunk before she checked the time. There were still a few hours until the orientation. Just as she was trying to figure out what to do to pass the time, the door opened, revealing a woman with pale skin and short red hair.

"Hey. Are you my new roomie?" she asked.

She nodded. "Looks like it. I'm Quinn."

"Quinn, nice to meet you. I'm Trina." She pulled in her bag and looked around. "This is much bigger than I thought it would be."

Quinn laughed. "Yeah, I thought that too. I took the bottom bunk if you don't mind, and I left the closet to the left open."

"Fine with me." They made small talk while Trina

unpacked. Trina had come from another culinary school in Colorado, but she had moved there from California.

"That's awesome," Quinn told her. "This is actually my first time seeing the ocean."

"Really?" Trina asked, clearly shocked.

Quinn laughed softly. "Really. I've never lived anywhere near the ocean, so I was excited when I received the offer."

"Well, we will definitely have to have a beach day when we have a day off," Trina decided, and Quinn smiled – she was definitely going to like it here.

After they'd both showered and dressed in their chef whites for orientation. Quinn tucked her long hair into a low bun and slicked it back to keep it out of her face.

Orientation was held in the main dining hall, all navy blue and gold with plush chairs and hardwood floors. The tables were pushed to the back, the chairs in rows. She found a spot right in the front as the room filled, eager to get started.

The meeting moved quickly. It was mainly to inform everyone what they could expect for the next week before guests arrived and some general housekeeping. Then, they were broken into our working clusters for the summer. Assessing her group, she realized her worst nightmare was coming true.

Brendon was there, in her group.

Quinn made a conscious effort to ignore him. Head Chef Westly, who she'd originally interviewed with, was leading her group. She looked up to him, so it was a dream to work under him.

"I expect everyone on my team to meet the highest of standards. I don't care if you're only prepping vegetables–I expect them to be perfect. Details are not to be overlooked, especially if you're even considering a job on board after you finish your schooling."

He went on to explain that every morning at four, all the kitchen staff would prep in the main galley. Then, they would break off into their individual assignments. Chef Westly spent most of his time in the main galley, serving the main courses. That was the place Quinn really wanted to be. Not only would they be welcoming guest chefs from all over the world, but they would also be cooking the cuisines of the places they docked. It would give her the chance to experience tons of different cooking methods she'd never see at home.

"Don't think that just because you ended up in my group, you're going to work in the main galley," he continued. "This week, we'll be cooking for the crew and learning menus. I expect you to treat this as if you were cooking for guests. After this week, I'll give out your assignments. I don't care who you are–don't think I won't put you on buffet duty. Prove to me you belong here. Any questions?" When no one spoke up, he nodded. "See you tomorrow morning."

"So together again, I guess," Brandon said as he sidled up to her. "Maybe we should meet up tonight. You know, study up."

"I'm fine studying by myself, thank you." Without a backwards glance, Quinn took her binder back to her room and got to work.

2

JORAH

Jorah leaned back from their desk, stretching their arms behind them. While they loved their job, doing admin work was the worst. They never thought owning their own business would be this boring. They always assumed being their own boss would be fun, and they wouldn't have to worry about things like this. They could hire an assistant, but they preferred to work from home, and didn't like having strangers in their space.

Their phone dinged on the desk, and they picked it up to find a text from Reka, telling them to come over ASAP. They called her instead. For someone who seemed to need their attention right away, it took her a long time to answer.

"I said come over, not call me," she said in lieu of hello.

"Some of us have jobs," they said, closing their laptop and stretching their tentacles under the desk.

"Oh please, real jobs are overrated. Come over, I need to show you something."

Jorah laughed. Even though they knew Reka worked hard as an artist, she always made jokes that she didn't have a real job. "Fine. Let me finish a few emails and then I'll be over."

They hung up, sent a few emails, and wandered over to her place. It was only a few blocks away; Jorah lived on an island called Damona, cut off from the human world, where paranormal beings could live openly. Even then, they were the only kraken living on the island. Krakens, by nature, were extremely independent and territorial. Krakens were few in numbers, and many mated based on strengthening their territory. Jorah was different, though. They didn't care about territory and hated solitude. They thrived in social settings and loved their plants and all their material possessions. So, even on an island full of non-humans, they were a bit of a spectacle. After so long, the interest had worn off, but sometimes, they could feel eyes on them still.

Soon, they were in front of Reka's door, which flew open before they could even knock.

"Geeze. Took you long enough," she snarked as she shut the door behind them. Reka, a water nymph with light blue skin and smaller fins for ears, had been Jorah's best friend for longer than anyone. Her father was a mage, so she had some human features other nymphs didn't, like her brown hair and freckles. Her hair was currently staked up with a paintbrush.

"I just finished this piece, and as soon as I was done, I knew it was for you."

Jorah followed her through her house that they had designed themselves. Unlike their home, which was a more Mediterranean style, her home was more eclectic, with jewel tones everywhere. They looked at her living room, thinking about adding a mirrored mosaic. One side held her paintings, but the other was mostly bare. Maybe an accented wall with printed wallpaper and a large mirror would be more appropriate than a mosaic. Those wavy ones were very on trend, and it would fit the vibe perfectly.

"Stop assessing my perfect home that I've already allowed you to rearrange a thousand times and follow me," Reka said, pulling them from their thoughts.

They huffed but followed her down the hall to her studio, a space Jorah had never touched. Reka insisted the walls be left white so nothing would interfere with her process. They didn't understand the method to her madness, but they didn't need to–her art spoke for itself.

"You ready?" she asked, walking over to the easel, a sheet draped over it like they were in a gallery. When they nodded, she tore it down to reveal something they weren't expecting: a colorful silhouette of a thick, feminine figure. She was facing away, holding her hair off her back. It was painted like a heat map, in different hues of red and orange, with a blue strip where a thong would sit. They couldn't explain it, but something about the figure felt familiar, almost like home. That didn't make any sense.

"I know it's not my style at all," she said, gesturing to her other paintings of landscapes with bright colors, "but it was like something inside wanted to make it. I don't know where you would put it, but it screamed you when I saw it."

They looked at it for a moment, thinking about where they could hang it. "Actually," they said, "I think this would go perfect in my bedroom." There was a space on the wall across from their bed just begging for *something*. They had been saving it for something special, and this felt special.

"Perfect! I'll wrap it up so you can take it with you. How's the hotel design going?"

They sighed loudly. "Just as well as you can expect with Kingsley. He's particular about every small detail, down to the color of the light switches. I understand it's supposed to be a luxury hotel, but he seriously needs to chill."

She laughed. "Isn't he, like, your highest paying client?"

They groaned. "Don't remind me. It's why I can let him go. Normally, I send him designs online, but since the project is here on the island, it feels like he's breathing even further down my neck."

"Aw, poor baby," Reka snarked, earning a middle finger from Jorah. "Come on–why don't we order take out and watch a movie? My treat."

"Fine, but only if we order something other than Mexican. We've had it like every time."

"But it's the perfect food," she whined.

Jorah snickered and smiled. "What about the Thai place down the block? You love their green curry."

She pouted but nodded. "Oh, and spring rolls!"

They laughed. "You got it."

3

QUINN

Prep week flew by in a storm of late nights and vegetable chopping. Every day, Quinn got up at three thirty to get to the kitchen fifteen minutes early, doing everything from inventory to prep work to dishes. Whatever she was asked to do, she did to the best of her abilities.

Every day, she was shuffled into a different restaurant on the boat, getting a feel for each area. In the afternoon, they normally had some sort of meeting or seminar discussing proper kitchen safety or emergency procedures. After dinner, they would meet with their chefs to discuss the day and learn about upcoming cuisines. Once she was off, she would sit in bed, studying her binder, making sure she was ready for whatever position she ended up in the next day.

Finally, Friday night rolled around, with guests arriving Monday. Tonight, they would get their assignments, then spend the weekend prepping. Quinn couldn't lie–she felt good after the week was up. She had worked hard and taken every piece of criticism she received to make herself better.

Even if she didn't end up in the main galley, she was at least confident she wouldn't end up on buffet duty.

They broke off into their groups, and everyone was on edge. Everyone except Brandon, that was. Being grouped with him this week was infuriating. He was constantly doing the bare minimum. He was normally late to morning prep, and he only did half the work everyone else was doing. On top of that, the work he *did* do was always sloppy. His knife cuts were never precise, and every station he prepped had missing items. Plus, he was always chatting with Chef Westley; apparently, his dad and Chef go skiing together every winter.

Chef finally joined them, sending the group into dead silence. "Listen up. I have everyone's assignments for the cruise. Remember that nothing is set in stone, and you could be moved at any time. Though I am who you report to, you need to listen to and get acquainted with the chef who runs the restaurant you'll be working in. Alright, let's get into it. Diaz and Smith, you'll be upstairs at Bao. Tisdale, you'll be working at Casa Luca's..."

Chef continued like that, assigning everyone to different spots. Finally, he announced, "Piker and Goddard, you'll be with me in the main galley. The rest of you are floaters, most likely working between the buffets and running prep food."

Quinn was gushing. She couldn't believe she'd made main galley. Samantha Goddard peered over at her and smiled; Quinn was just thrilled she wasn't paired with a slacker. Chef was continuing with instructions when he was suddenly interrupted.

"I'm sorry, Chef, you forgot to call Cotley," Brandon said.

"I didn't. You're part of the floater team," Chef replied.

"But that doesn't make sense. You know who my dad is. I can't be expected to-"

Chef cut him off. "If you have an issue with your placement, we can speak after the meeting. I placed people based on their skills this past week, nothing more."

Brandon stood there with his mouth agape, and Quinn had to cover her mouth to hide her amusement. Once the meeting was over, Brandon pulled Chef Westley aside and they got into it.

Not wanting to see how *that* shitshow would pan out, Quinn scurried back to her room, excited to study up on the first menu for the main galley.

Quinn's weekend consisted of learning the first menu and the ins and outs of the kitchen. Dinner was the main meal served there, with five courses every night. The menu for now reflects the first stop, Hawaii. While Quinn loved the Saimin dish the most, she was tasked with making Croissada pastries, sort of like croissants but covered in sugar and filled with Bavarian cream. Pastries weren't her favorite thing to make, but Croissada were soft and fluffy and delicious.

Brandon had been sulking around, still showing up late and being essentially useless. Even with his uselessness, by Monday, we're all ready to go, and the first service goes off without a hitch. Everyone in the main galley was efficient and put together; Quinn had to work hard to keep up, but by the end of the night, she felt incredible.

As she was walking down the hall to her room, she saw

Brandon coming the other way, his chef whites covered in red sauce. "Hey, you okay?"

"What's it to you?" he retorted.

She held her hands up. "Never mind then."

He pushed past her, and she continued to her room, finding Trina there, brushing out her wet hair.

Trina smiled as Quinn pushed into the room and closed the door behind her. "Hey! How was your first day?"

She sighed a dreamy, happy sigh. "Amazing! It was everything I could have imagined and more. What about you?"

Since Trina was a pastry chef, she was assigned to the patisserie on the main deck. "Great. We're making tons of strawberry mochi, and it's been the best." Trina paused for a moment. "Hey, you know the blonde guy in your group? The tall one?"

Quinn quirked a brow. "You mean Brandon?"

"Yeah, him. I guess he was working at the children's build-your-own-pizza place, and some kid threw a fit and knocked a whole container of sauce on him. I saw the whole thing."

Quinn fell into a fit of laughter. "*That's* why he was covered in sauce in the hall! We go to the same school, and he's the worst. He's Chef Cotley's son."

Trina's eyes went big. "You mean the world-famous Chef Cotley who's opened restaurants all over the country?"

"The very one. That's why he expects everything to be handed to him. It's nice to see him struggle for a change."

"Oh, he's definitely struggling." They burst into a fit of laughter.

The week flew by, and finally, they docked in Hawaii. Quinn was ridiculously excited–they were going to watch Chef Māhoe make lau lau, a traditional Hawaiian dish with pork and butterfish steamed in lu'au leaves and ti leaves.

Chef Māhoe's workshop was incredible, and Quinn loved every moment. The fish and pork combo was amazing, and Quinn learned so much. Chef Māhoe even complimented her leaf folding technique.

When the workshop ended, Quinn got right back to prepping for dinner service. As she was chopping up carrots, Chef Westley asked to speak with her privately.

"Piker, you have been excellent these past few weeks. I was worried when Chef Tramis reached out. I thought maybe she owed someone a favor to put a good word in, but you're obviously the real deal. Even Chef Māhoe gave you praise. I want you to start shadowing me. You definitely have what it takes to run a kitchen, and I want you to experience it first-hand."

Quinn quickly realized her jaw was on the floor and promptly shut it. "T-that would be amazing. I would be honored, Chef."

Chef Westley smiled. "Please, the honor is mine. Honestly, I'm hoping this experience will convince you to take the job after school. I'm sure many of our guest chefs will try to scoop you up, just as sure I am that we'll be offering you a job."

Quinn was again left speechless. All she could do was smile and nod.

"Perfect," he continued. "Why don't you take the rest of the afternoon off? You've been here longer than anyone and haven't stepped foot outside yet. Go enjoy it. Meet me in my office in the morning."

"Yes, Chef," she responded, then almost skipped her way back to her room. On her way, she noticed Brandon glaring at her, and all she could do was smile back.

Quinn quickly changed into her bathing suit and a white, lacy cover up to head out to the beach. The warm ocean air fluttered through her hair as she padded down the dock, the sun setting, coloring the sky in beautiful purples and pinks.

She walked down to the ocean and stared at the clear water in front of her. She had never been in the ocean, and what a more perfect place to start than Hawaii? Quinn waded into the water, letting her toes wiggle in the wet sand. The waves crashed over her feet, and she stood there, soaking it all in.

It felt like her dreams were finally happening; everything she'd ever worked for was coming together. With that, she sat in the ocean and thought about her future.

4

JORAH

A tug.

Jorah felt a tug from their chest, pulling them to the ocean, one strong enough to wake them at this god-awful hour. It wasn't the normal connection they felt with the ocean, the one always lying right below the surface. As a kraken, a deep connection with the ocean was a given, but this was different, stronger. What was it?

Whatever it was felt important, like they needed to jump up and go. *Now*. Though this feeling was unfamiliar, they had learned a long time ago that the ocean knew things. It was pointless to question it.

Jorah moved from their bedroom to the balcony overlooking the ocean and stared out into the expanse. The instant feeling to go never wavered, but to where? They weren't sure, but the need was bone deep.

They moved back to the bedroom, threw on a day robe, and rushed down the street to Reka. They knocked hard, feeling extremely impatient. After a painfully long wait, she opened the door. "Oh my god, Jor, do you know what time it is?"

"I need to leave. I don't know how long I'll be gone, but can you watch the townhouse until I return? Water my plants?"

Reka crossed her arms and leaned against the frame. "What are you talking about Jor? It's like seven in the morning. I've never seen you up this early."

They shook their head. "I need to leave. The ocean is... calling me. I don't know how to explain it, but I need to go."

"Jor, you sound crazy. Come on, why don't you come in for some coffee, and we'll talk this out?"

Jorah stepped back. "No, Re. I need to leave now. I'll return soon, I promise."

She stared at them for a moment. "You're serious? How do you even know where you're going?"

"The ocean will guide me."

She let out a loud sigh. "Fine, whatever. If this is some kind of...*you* thing, then go, but please be careful."

"I promise I will," Jorah said with a soft smile.

"Oh, and when you get back, we should meet up with my parents. They miss you."

Jorah nodded before turning to leave. Not only did they really need to get going, but they also found themselves uncomfortable with the thought of someone...missing them. They had lived on this island for a very long time, but it was still weird to think about having parental figures around.

They moved to the beach, leaving their robe in one of the cubby slots set up nearby. Since a lot of ocean-dwelling beings took up residence on this island, it was normal for people to take off their garments and have a swim. Modesty wasn't a big issue in the paranormal world like it was for humans, so no one batted an eye. Even though they were the only one out there at this awful hour.

Jorah jumped into the water, feeling their body come to life as they dove. Though they loved living on their little island, the ocean made them feel alive.

They swam hard in the direction of the pull, hoping that whatever they found was worth it.

5

QUINN

The few days Quinn spent in Hawaii were paradise. The weather was warm, the ocean incredible. All too soon, though, the ship was heading toward Samoa. After her day off, she showed up to Chef Westley's office for shadowing. She got to sit in on meetings with head chefs, where they discussed upcoming menus, and checked in with other restaurants on the ship.

A week went by like a fever dream, and it felt like everything was falling into place. After a long night of dinner service, Quinn finally made her way back to her room, where Trina sat cross legged in front of their mirror, putting on mascara.

"There you are," she chirped, standing quickly. "There's going to be an intern party tonight. It's at one of the day bars on the deck; you have to come!"

Quinn sighed. "I don't think so. I'm exhausted."

Trina grabbed her hand. "Oh, come on. You're only young once, and I'm sure you can miss out on a couple hours of sleep. It will be fun." Quinn quirked her eyebrow at her, but Trina was relentless. "Come on. Just an hour."

"Okay." Quinn looked up, surprised the word had just come out of her mouth.

Trina squealed. "Awesome. Get dressed and we'll go."

Quinn opened her drawers and pulled out a sage green summer dress. It was one of the nicer things she owned, with spaghetti straps and lace detailing toward the bottom. She threw on some mascara and brow gel before pulling her brown strands down and quickly brushing them out.

The party was at one of the bars toward the back of the boat, on one of the upper levels. Since it was only open during the day, it seemed they let the interns enjoy some party time. Quinn ordered some tropical drink that tasted like pineapples and orange juice, then headed to the dance floor with Trina, meeting up with a bunch of people who worked in the patisserie. They danced and chatted, and Quinn actually found herself having fun.

Eventually, she grew hot and tired, and she decided to go out to the deck. She leaned against the railing, letting the cool ocean air move through her hair.

Suddenly, a slurred voice came from behind her. "Well, if it isn't little miss perfect."

She turned to see Brandon swaying behind her. She ignored him, like always, looking back over the side.

"Oh, come on, Quinn, don't be like that. We all know you're sucking Chef's cock. Must be pretty good, too, considering he made you his protégé. Can I get some too? I'll set you up in one of my dad's restaurants, easy."

Anger bubbled to the surface of her chest, and she lashed out. "No, Brandon. I don't need to stoop to things like that to move up in the world. I'm just talented."

"Oh, so now you think you're better than me or something?" he asked, slowly moving closer. "Don't forget that I'm a Cotley, and I *will* be a great chef."

"Yeah, whatever." He was almost on top of her now, and she could smell the alcohol lingering on his breath. "Get away from me, Brandon."

"No, you stupid bitch. I'm tired of your attitude. I'm tired of you taking my rightful place. *I'm* supposed to be his protégé, not some worthless whore." He pushed up against her roughly, and she fought back, trying to get away. She tried calling out to the bar, but it was too far, the music too loud.

"Stop," she screeched, but he wasn't listening.

Suddenly, she tried to push around him, and he shoved her hard. With her push, she careened over the edge, falling toward the water. She screamed and tried to reach for the boat, but it was no use.

It felt like she was falling forever, but also no time at all. She hit the water with a smack, the air leaving her lungs in a whoosh. She struggled, trying to swim upward; at least, what she hoped was upward. Her lungs burned, and eventually, she felt her consciousness slip away.

6

JORAH

J orah swam fast, their tentacles making quick work through the water. The call pulling at them had since disappeared, but they followed anyway, hoping whatever it was was still there.

They were about halfway when the tug came back, this time much harder, much closer. Jorah switched directions, moving swiftly through the water. The tug felt more urgent, like something was wrong. They pushed harder, moving as fast as possible.

Eventually, they saw something small, flailing in the water for a moment and then stopping. They rushed forward and wrapped their tentacles around the...human? Why had the ocean pulled them to a human? Jorah quickly moved to the surface, raising the human's face above water.

Jorah hadn't had any interaction with humans in many years, but they were sure they couldn't breathe in water.

Looking closely, Jorah realized they must have fallen off the boat cruising along in front of them. Did the human fall? Should they put it back?

No. Mine.

The thought was involuntary but final. Looking down, they took in the human's long, dark hair and round cheeks, their head lulled back and unmoving. Jorah moved closer, relieved to find she was breathing.

Without much further thought, Jorah set off back toward home with the human, swimming on the top of the water to allow her to breathe. After a few moments, they stopped, realizing they couldn't take her home. Humans weren't allowed on Damona. Quickly formulating a plan, they changed course, heading to a small island a short distance away from the main one.

Along with Damona, there were other, smaller islands along the edges that fell under the same protection, most of them used for beach houses. Jorah occupied one themselves. It was small and the furthest one from the main isle. They had a small home built there a while ago. While they loved the main island, there were times they needed to get away. Though they weren't as independent as other krakens, they still liked having space.

Jorah switched course and headed there instead. It took a while, but they finally walked them up on shore. The beach wasn't as pristine as it was on the mainland, but the sand was still soft. They walked quickly to their home; it was a bit smaller than the one on the mainland, but still comfortable.

Looking at the human in their arms more closely, they noticed she had brown hair and bronzed skin. Her lashes were long and thick, her face rounded. They thought about what color her eyes must be. She wore a green dress that was now partially see through due to the water, showcasing her soft skin, so unlike theirs, which was firmer in texture. Her entire body was softer in their hold; they thought about holding her hips in a much different way, but quickly shook away the thought, knowing they needed to focus.

Jorah quickly moved to their kitchen, formulating a plan. They obviously wanted the human to stay, but humans weren't allowed on Damona. They knew who to ask, but they weren't excited about it.

Checking on the human one more time to ensure they were still asleep, they gave Reka a call. She answered immediately.

"Hey Jor. I've been wondering how long you'd be gone. I watered all your plants. I even fed the weird one that eats meat. So," she started, not letting them get a word in, as usual, "did you find out what this big mystery draw was?"

They took a deep breath. "I did."

"Okay... and?"

"I believe she is my fated one."

It sounded like Reka had spit out her tea. Jorah understood the feeling–it was the first time they'd said it out loud, but it was the only thing that made sense. "Are you sure?"

"It's the only thing I can think of. The ocean drew me right to her, and when I reached her, there was this pull I don't think could be described in any other way."

It sounded like Reka was about to spontaneously combust on the other end. "I'm so happy for you! I need to meet her immediately. Shit, my place is a mess. Hold on, give me an hour."

Jorah interrupted her before she could get any farther. "She's human."

There was a long pause on the other end. "I'm sorry. What?"

"She seemed to have fallen off a large ship. I saved her, but she was definitely who I was drawn to."

Reka sounded suddenly wary. "So where is she?"

Jorah let out a long breath. "At the beach house."

"Jor. You know no humans are allowed here."

"I know, I know, but I couldn't just leave her."

Reka sighed, louder this time. "Okay, here's the plan: I'll go talk to mom and see if she can help us get everything sorted. Then, I want to meet this person."

Jorah nodded, even though they knew Reka couldn't see it. "You will, I promise."

"Fine. I'll call you with updates, but you better call me, too."

"I will." Getting off the phone, Jorah slumped down at their desk. All they could do now was wait for the human to wake.

7

QUINN

Quinn awoke to the sounds of the ocean. She had a terrible dream. She went to a party with Trina and got into a fight with Brandon. Then, he pushed her into the...

She shot up, feeling the plush blankets around her, finally noticing the tight feeling of her skin from the salt water. Brandon *had* pushed her into the ocean. What happened? Where was she?

Looking around, she found herself in a mostly white bedroom, accented with pops of wood and green. It was the most styled bedroom she'd ever seen, but she needed to focus.

She stood and moved to the side, where a large, flowy curtain draped down from the ceiling. Pulling it back, she found a balcony overlooking the ocean, but it wasn't like the one in Hawaii. The sand was lighter, the ocean bluer. There were no other buildings or people around, at least that she could see.

"You're awake," a melodic voice said behind her.

She immediately dropped the curtain and turned with a

start, and her eyes widened as she took in the being in front of her. They looked a bit like a giant squid at the bottom, with bluish green skin and tentacles. Their top half was still blue, but it had a more human look. They had arms that were currently crossed, their shoulder leaning against the door frame. Though their face was made up of sharp planes, there was a softness to their green eyes. On top of their head sat what looked like two, thin tendrils that fell behind them, that looked almost like horns. There were some smaller looking ones of different lengths surrounding their head, almost like a crown.

She should be scared. Quinn knew she should be shaking un fear, but she felt none. Maybe she was in shock. After all, she was just pushed off a cruise ship. "What happened to me?"

"I saved you, human," they said. "It seems you were... displaced from your ship."

"That's one way to say it." She rubbed her eyes a bit too hard, trying to process what was happening. "Where are we?"

"My home. Well, my beach home. I am Jorah, and I use they/them pronouns. Who are you?"

She considered saying nothing, but then she decided it would be better to remain cordial. "I'm Quinn. I go with she/her."

Jorah moved to the chair on the other side of the room and settled in, their tentacles spilling over the edges.

"Thank you for saving me," she said, "but is there any way you could take me back? I need to go back." She had to go back to school and finish her internship. Will people know Brandon pushed her? How would she explain it all?

"I'm afraid I can't."

Quinn's eyes went big. "What?"

"I saved you. That means you owe me a life debt."

She blinked at them. "A what?"

"I saved your life, meaning until I'm repaid, you are to stay here."

Quinn digested that information. She couldn't just be expected to stay here. "But I have an internship to get back to, a life. You can't just take me from it."

A look Quinn couldn't place crossed their face briefly, but it was gone in an instant. They said nothing, just continuing to look at her.

She felt her anger rise. "I'm telling you, I can't stay here. People will look for me."

"People will assume you died, and you very well could have."

She flinched. They were right. No one would expect her back. They would assume she was gone. Would they send a search party? Would Brandon tell them what happened? "Okay, so what do I do until then?"

"You may stay here. I have a spare room and will provide you with anything you need."

"How the hell am I supposed to repay you a life debt? You're a..." she trailed off. She had no idea what they were.

Their mouth tilted in a slight grin, but it quickly vanished. "I am a kraken. Don't worry–I'll find a way for you to repay it. For now, just stay here."

She narrowed her eyes but said nothing. What could she say? They were a kraken; she knew she wouldn't be able to get very far with them around. She would have to bide her time until she was able to escape. "Can I at least have a shower?" she asked.

"Of course." Jorah moved with grace, almost floating across the floor to the closet. They pulled out a large piece of fabric that looked like green silk and a towel and put them on the bed. "The washroom is through that door. Let me know if you need anything else. You can come out whenever you're done." With that, they left by the door they came through.

Once they left, Quinn tried to open the door to the patio and found it miraculously open. She stepped out, and the sound of waves crashing doubled. She could see the beach close below, the smell of the ocean wafting to her on the breeze and engulfing her. She looked down–she was at least three floors up, and there was nothing close enough to jump to. She could tie a bedsheet around the banister and climb down, but she didn't trust herself enough to tie a good knot. Plus, then what? Maybe this was good. Jorah didn't seem like they wanted to hurt her, just somehow repay an entire life debt. No pressure. She had some time to think about what to do next, and maybe when she got back, she could talk to Chef Westly and keep working on the ship.

With that plan in mind, she moved to the bathroom. It had a completely different feel from the bedroom, all black everything with industrial style lights. Across from it was the largest bath she'd ever seen, and a standing shower on the other side that was also giant. She examined the bath and thought about taking one, but she ultimately decided to go for a shower.

Peeling off her dress, she quickly showered then put on the clothes she was given. It wasn't like anything she'd worn before, and it swallowed her whole. It looked like a giant sheet of silk with two slits going all the way down the sides and straps wrapping around either side. She wore it like a wrap dress, using the bands to tie it tightly around her waist. There were still the two giant slits up the sides, but she kind of liked it.

When she was done, she ventured out the door Jorah

came through earlier. She walked down the stairs, only to be met with a large open concept living room and kitchen almost overrun with plants. They were growing everywhere: leafy vines climbed the walls, and colorful flowers grew along the windowsill. She didn't know much about plants, but it was very pretty. The kitchen, though, was beautiful. There were tons of cabinets and a full gas range stove. The fridge was massive, and there was enough counter space for four people to work easily.

I wonder if they'll let me cook something in there.

As she was drooling over the kitchen, she noticed Jorah perched on one of the island stools, looking at a tablet. Or, at least, they were. Now, their eyes were trained on her, a heat simmering there that confused her, but she decided to ignoreOkay it for now.

"Are you feeling better?" they asked, and she nodded. "Good. Would you like food? I don't keep much here, but I can whip something up."

"I can cook," she said, walking around the island.

"Please, I do not mind."

They met her on the other side of the island, bringing them toe to toe–er, tentacle to toe. She knew they were very close, and she felt strange butterflies in her gut, even though that was *ridiculous*.

"I prefer to cook," she said. "It's what I do."

Their expression softened at her insistence, conceding quicker than she expected. "If that is what you truly want."

"It is." They nodded and backed off, moving back to the other side of the island.

Quinn began looking around the kitchen, trying to figure out what to make. What does a kraken eat? "Do you have any preferences?"

Jorah shifted uncomfortably. "You don't need to worry about me."

Quinn quirked her head to the side. "Why? Do you not eat?"

"No, I do."

"Great. What kinds of things?"

They again looked unsure. "We eat a lot of fish on the island, but I am fine with anything."

With a nod, she took stock of the kitchen. They really didn't keep much here, but there seemed to be some mahi mahi, vegetables, and some flour. She set to work quickly, falling into an easy rhythm, learning the kitchen. It almost felt normal, but she had no idea why. Ignoring that odd sensation, she put up her hair and got to work.

8

JORAH

Jorah watched Quinn dance around the kitchen like she belonged there. It made their heart sing seeing her fit into their space so perfectly. They had bought a ton of stuff for their kitchen here. They didn't know why at the time–it had just felt right to buy a bunch of random appliances and kitchen equipment. They ordered out for almost every meal, but still insisted on owning a pristine knife set and tortilla press.

They watched as she mixed and pressed dough while simultaneously cooking fish and prepping vegetables. Even though she worked vigorously and efficiently, she looked happy and carefree, and that almost made their little lie worth it.

Almost.

When they saw her and she mentioned leaving, their chest tightened with the need to keep her there. They thought about returning her, but they couldn't bring themselves to do it. When Jorah was a child, their mother told them an old folk tale about krakens who used to save humans and make them repay the debt by essentially becoming indentured servants. While Jorah had no plans to force Quinn to do anything, it was the first thing that sprang to mind. They didn't know what they would say if she asked what she owed, but they hoped they could tell her the truth before that happened. They just needed time to impress her, maybe even woo her.

Since they've had this thought, the fear they would be a bad fated one sat heavily on their chest. Krakens by nature didn't care for things that didn't benefit them personally. And while they didn't want to be like that, how were they supposed to fight their own genetics? They felt the need to prove themselves, not only to Quinn, but to themselves, and starting with such a huge act of selfishness didn't bode well.

"Here," Quinn said, snapping them out of their thoughts. She set a plate down in front of them, four tacos on it with salsa and some kind of green sauce, identical to her own plate.

They took a bite and moaned aloud. "Holy shit," they said around the bite, "this is this best thing I've ever eaten."

Looking at Quinn, they could see heat working its way across her cheeks. "It's just some tacos," she mumbled, looking at her own food.

Jorah reached across the island and took her hand. "Do not discount your talent. I have had many meals prepared by chefs centuries older than you, and I'm not lying when I say even from something this simple, I can tell you have something special."

She turned even redder, the blush flowing down to her neck and chest. They'd noticed when she came out that she wore her robe in an interesting way. It was meant for a body like theirs, so it makes sense that it wouldn't quite fit, but the way she had it wrapped hugged her luscious curves creating almost a dress. There were slits up each side, showing plenty of thigh when she walked. It made their mouth water in a way that had nothing to do with the food.

"Well...thanks." She looked to where their hands touched, and they pulled back, suddenly feeling self-conscious. To their surprise, she seemed to reach out for a fraction of a second before pulling back. Jorah was given a little hope when she didn't immediately scream and run upon meeting them, but they still worried about her rejection. They ate in relative silence, but it didn't feel uncomfortable. Once they'd finished, Quinn started picking up their plate, along with hers.

"What are you doing?" they asked, brows furrowed.

She froze in place, looking up at them confused. "Cleaning the giant mess I just created."

"No. You just cooked. Sit and relax. I will clean."

She shook her head. "It's fine. I'm used to doing the clean up after."

They stood, moving around to where she stood. "Not here. Let me do the cleaning. You just cooked us an entire meal. Sit."

She looked like she wanted to argue, but luckily, she didn't. She just relaxed back into her seat while they took their plates to the sink and started cleaning.

9

QUINN

Quinn watched as Jorah made their way around the counter to clean. She hadn't realized she'd made such a mess until she watched them clean it. For someone who didn't cook, Jorah had everything a chef could ever want. She could tell they put a lot of work into their home, right down to the stainless-steel pans that made her mouth water. She tried to do what they asked, but it was next to impossible. There was no way she could just sit there and watch them work while she did nothing.

She jumped up and came around the island to help. They were putting some dishes up on a high shelf, and she watched as their muscles flexed, their robe falling a bit down one shoulder.

Last year, she had a roommate who was really into romance novels. Quinn didn't have time for them, but one day, while she was cleaning, she picked one up and skimmed it. The skimming quickly turned into a full-on read, but she hadn't picked up one since. There were things in there she didn't expect, including some tentacle scenes.

She hadn't thought about it much since then, but the memories of all the ways those tentacles were used came flooding back now.

She looked up at them and noticed they were staring back, watching her. "I wasn't staring," she said, feeling her face flush.

Yeah, that sounded legit.

"Sure," they said with a smirk.

"No, I mean, not because you're not human. I was just thinking about..." She trailed off. She couldn't say tentacle sex, because that's how you make your prison guard angry. Still, she didn't want them to think she was staring because they were a kraken. She wasn't afraid of them, oddly enough. "The plates," she said suddenly. "I just love those plates. They're such a nice color."

They only smirked and turned back to placing things in their cabinets. Quinn's face turned beet red, and she quickly averted her eyes. She figured she should get to work and stop embarrassing herself, so she reached for a pan, but it was quickly snatched from her hand. Jorah didn't even turn in her direction; they had picked up the pan with another tentacle, and she was instantly back to thinking about how handy they must be.

She picked up a glass, but that was also quickly plucked from her hands. And again with the spatula.

"I could do this all day," they said, still facing the cupboard.

Quinn huffed her annoyance. "I'm just helping a bit," she said, grabbing a spoon.

Again, Jorah swooped it out of her hand. "Thank you, but I don't need your help, sirenita. You already cooked an excellent meal. I'll clean up, and you will relax."

Did they just call her something in Spanish? She shook

it off, assuming it was an accident. "It's fine. I made a bigger mess than I needed to, and I wouldn't want..." She yelped as she was suddenly lifted off the ground and swept away. Jorah had picked her up, moving her away from the kitchen.

"Why did you do that?" she huffed. Their arms were around her, and two tentacles curled around her bottom, but it felt more like a caress than a restraining hold.

They brought her all the way to the living room, plopping her down on the plush couch. It was a really deep couch, probably to fit tentacles comfortably. "I appreciate your help, but I am very capable of running a dishwasher. So, you sit and relax. You can watch whatever you want." Jorah picked up a throw blanket and tossed it on top of her. "Stay."

"What am I, a dog?" she asked. She tried to put some bite behind it, but failed miserably.

"No, you look very different from a canine." She stared at them blankly, and they laughed, returning those strange butterflies to her belly. "I'm joking. Now, relax."

They moved back to the kitchen, and Quinn flicked on the TV. She was surprised to see all the normal shows she would expect, plus some others she'd never seen. She found one of her favorite cooking shows and hunkered down.

After cleaning, Jorah came and sat with her, watching the show and asking questions. Normally, she found that annoying. People usually only asked because they wanted to know if the people on TV actually knew how to cook and weren't just actors. Jorah, on the other hand, seemed genuinely interested in the technique and how she would do it. When they watched a show where the contestants were given a random bag of ingredients, Jorah seemed to notice Quinn was irritated about a contestant's use of pineapple. It almost freaked her out how perceptive they seemed, but some people were more empathetic, so she just chalked it up to that.

The entire experience felt so...domestic, and yet she hadn't freaked out yet. She expected she would at some point, but the panic never came, which should also make her panic. She should be multiple levels of panic deep, but all she felt was a steady calm.

After a few episodes, Jorah turned to her. "Would you like a tour of the house?"

"Sure." Maybe she could find another escape route. She still wasn't sure how she would get off the island, but one struggle at a time.

Jorah showed her through the house. It was all a bit confusing, with each room having a completely different aesthetic. There was a downstairs bathroom with a 70's retro vibe, and a home office with a clean and modern vibe. They didn't specify their job, but Quinn spied pages scattered around that looked like sketches, and a drawing tablet on the desk. Last downstairs was a gorgeous, enclosed patio. The front wall and ceiling were both made of glass, with thick, black metal pieces between each pane. The room had a more industrial feel to it, with fairy lights strewn across the ceiling and patinated metal furniture. There was a door leading directly out into the beach, and even at night, you could see the whites of the waves.

Soon, they moved back up the stairs. Photos lined the walls, but she didn't stop long enough to really look at them. She recognized the room she came out of but noticed a door across the hall.

"This will be the room you stay in," they said when they finally stopped. The room had an ethereal vibe, with a golden, four-poster bed covered in emerald-green curtains. Behind the bed was mosaic wallpaper with green and gold swirls. All the furniture in the room matched, and there's a television in a gold frame sitting on an ornamental vanity.

"I'm staying here?" she asked, looking around, eyes wide.

"Yes, if you'd like. I can always change things if you're unhappy." Their eyes seemed to be bouncing around, as if searching for flaws.

Instead, Quinn looked around in awe. She had never seen a room this opulent. It looked like it was pulled straight out of a Pinterest board. "It's stunning. I've never seen a room so gorgeous. Honestly, this whole house is amazing. Whoever designed it did an excellent job."

She could have sworn their chest puffed up a bit. "I did. I'm an interior designer."

Her gaze turned to Jorah. "Really?"

"Yes. I've designed things all over the island I live on. Houses, businesses, you name it. This is kind of my tester house. Every room is so different because it gives me a chance to try out new stuff."

Quinn was impressed. It made sense with their office, but this really felt next level. Even though each room was different, it all felt oddly cohesive.

She yawned loudly, the absurdity of the day finally catching up to her. "I think I'm going to go to bed, if that's okay."

They nodded. "Of course. Please let me know if you need anything else."

Quinn smiled at them, and they smiled back. Their smile warmed her belly and started those damn butterflies again. She was going to need to get them a cage.

Without another word, Jorah slipped out of the room and closed the door. Quinn locked the door before turning back to the room. It's not like she thought they would do anything. For someone who was basically holding her captive, she felt strangely like she could trust them. She just wanted to feel like she had some control.

Quinn walked to the window, opening it so she could hear the ocean waves crashing outside. She couldn't even hear that when she was on the boat. Deciding to leave her robe on, she hopped into the bed. It was plusher than it looked, and she all but sank down into it. She fell asleep sleep faster than she ever had, drifting off to the sounds of the ocean.

10

JORAH

Jorah woke with a start the next morning, hearing rustling coming from outside. Glancing at the clock, they realized it was eight in the morning. Before everything with Quinn, they never got up before ten. It was the main perk of owning their own business. They threw on a gold robe and moved to see what the noise was.

Jorah had spent more time researching humans and the things they needed when Quinn excused herself the night before. After they were sure she was asleep, they went to the main island to buy clothes and get more groceries and any cooking supplies they didn't have. Ele, the selkie who ran the clothing store, was suspicious of their request, but they were one of her best customers, so she didn't question it much. They were able to pick up a few ready-made pieces, but Ele promised to have the rest delivered in a few days.

Then, they went to a cooking supplies store in town and bought everything they didn't have that she could possibly need. After eating her food and watching those cooking shows, they knew she had something special. What kind of fated one would they be if they didn't do everything they could to help her succeed?

Jorah entered the kitchen to find Quinn with her back turned, pulling something out of the oven–whatever it was smelled amazing. From the back, they could see her round ass bounce as she shut the oven. She was wearing the flowing green pants and black tank top they'd left her last night. It put all her curves on display and showed a small strip of skin on her belly. They had to keep their thoughts under control. These silk robes did nothing to hide an erection.

When she turned around, she almost dropped her pan with a start. "Geez, you scared me," she huffed, setting the pan on the stove. "Not because of, you know...I mean, just because I didn't hear you coming, no other reason."

Jorah smiled at her. They could tell she wasn't afraid of them being a kraken. In fact, even when they first met, they sensed no fear from her. They weren't as large as the krakens depicted in the media, obviously, but they were still very different, and yet, she seemed unbothered. "It is fine. I do move rather quietly."

"Well, I made breakfast if you want anything. You have such cool stuff in your kitchen. Did you go grocery shopping last night? I don't remember it being so well stocked."

"I picked up a few extra things. Plus, I had some things ordered. I believe a deep fryer and an ice cream machine are being delivered in a few days."

She looked at them with her mouth wide. "I- well, thank you. You didn't have to do all this."

"Don't worry about it. I have no shortage of money and want you to have everything you could need while you're here." *And hope that you will stay.* They didn't voice that part out loud. It was too soon. They had to first prove they would be a good partner.

Her cheeks reddened, and she looked away. "Well, thank you. Dig in."

When they finally pulled their attention from Quinn, they realized just how much food was there. There was an egg dish with refried beans and other veggies, bread with frosting on top, and a plate loaded with sausages. "This is quite the spread." They grabbed a plate.

"Yeah. Sorry if it's a bit much. I made huevos rancheros, which is objectively the best egg dish there is. Oh, and a french toast bread pudding. Normally, I would use challah bread, but I saw you had brioche and decided to try that."

They finished filling one plate and handed it to her before loading up the next. "Oh, thanks." Her surprise about simple decency like making her plate or cleaning after she cooked a massive meal didn't sit well with them. They wanted her to feel cared for, and it was obviously not something she was used to.

They would need to change that.

They ate in a comfortable silence, the food equally as delicious as the night before. When they said so, she reddened once more and claimed the french toast would have been better if she had time to make her own bread. They couldn't see what else could make this decadent treat better, but she was clearly the expert, so they remained silent.

Once they finished, Jorah felt like they were going to have to roll around the rest of the day. Their morning meal usually consisted of toast with jam, or overcooked scrambled eggs, if they were feeling up for it. Most were surprised a kraken ate anything except raw fish. It's what they ate for a long time, but once they moved to the island and tried more of what dry land had to offer, they were obsessed. This topped almost anything else they'd had.

Quinn once again got up and tried to start cleaning, but they caught her before she got far. It reminded them of when they picked her up and took her to the couch yesterday. When they picked her up, it was an unconscious reaction. Her warmth had soaked through their tentacles, making them never want to release her, and they were pleasantly surprised when she didn't recoil or shy away. It actually felt like she leaned into their touch, which gave them further hope.

"I'll clean," they said when she turned to them.

"But you have to work," she argued, although she made no move to get up.

They shuffled her plate across the island toward the sink. "Don't worry. I normally don't start until around noon, so I'm way ahead of schedule."

She looked like she wanted to argue but sat back down instead. They got up and started washing dishes and putting everything away. "So, do you have to go to an office or something?" she asked.

"No. I work for myself, so I have a home office. Later this week, I need to go on site to a new hotel, but I work from home for the most part. Were you working on the ship before..." they asked, trailing off. Jorah wasn't sure if they should bring it up, but they wanted to know more.

Her face contorted for a moment before going back to neutral. "Yes. I'm going to school to be a chef, and you need to do an internship to graduate. This cruise was one of the most sought-after internships, with only a few spots."

Jorah's chest swelled with pride for their fated one. "With your skill, it is no surprise you got it."

Her face heated, and she shrugged. "I just put in the work."

"I do not doubt that, but you are also talented, and that cannot be taught."

She again looked away, but this time, with a small smile on her face. She obviously wasn't used to compliments and Jorah planned on changing that. They finished putting the dishes in the dishwasher and washed their hands. "By the way, thank you for the clothes," she said. "They fit very well."

"Of course. Let me know if there is anything else you need and I will provide it for you." She nodded and they continued. "Well, you have free roam of the house. You may go to the beach if you'd like. It's private, so no one should bother you."

She blinked at them. "I can go outside?"

Jorah looked out, checking once again to ensure it was safe. "Yes. Why wouldn't you?"

"Aren't you worried about me running away from life debt or whatever?" Her face betrayed that she hadn't meant to say that, but she stared at them for an answer, nonetheless.

They recovered quickly. "Well, unless you can swim to the closest human island, which is well over 3,000 miles away, I don't think you're going anywhere. Oh, and there's a magical barrier between my land and the next. People pay top dollar to live here, and they value their privacy."

Jorah could see the determination settling on her face, almost as if they had offered her a challenge. They weren't concerned, though. While she was determined, those barriers were no joke, and she wasn't foolish enough to think she could swim the distance. "Well, I'll be in my office. Let me know if you need anything."

They brushed past her and made their way to their office. Taking one last peek, they noticed her smiling softly.

11

QUINN

Jorah left for their office, leaving Quinn at a loss of what to do. She knew she went overboard with breakfast, but seeing the kitchen stocked with nearly every ingredient imaginable made her giddy. Plus, it was obvious they went somewhere while she slept, considering there were clothes made for her body type and even more groceries were in the pantry.

It made her heart flutter seeing Jorah go through all this trouble for her. No one had ever done anything like this for her. As a former foster child, she was used to receiving hand me downs, and there were usually so many kids, there wasn't enough attention to go around. She had dated a little, but it normally fizzled out, or there were red flags she had blatantly ignored in the beginning.

Even though Jorah was kind to her, she had to keep her head on straight. She had no idea what paying back a life debt entailed, and she couldn't forget they were keeping her here against her will. If that wasn't a red flag, she didn't know what was.

She moved back to the kitchen. She thought about going

outside but decided against it for now. Maybe she could later, but it felt odd not to do any type of work. She opted to make lunch for her and Jorah whenever they were done. Once that got going, she started some bread, and soon moved on to pastries.

Hours must have gone by. By the time she looked up, the sun was setting. She was a bit worried–Jorah hadn't come out of their office since the morning. She had the lunch wrapped up in the fridge, but they didn't come to eat. Quinn knew it was ridiculous to be worried about her captor, but she couldn't help it. She was a worrier, and it had nothing to do with the fact that they seemed to actually care about her. That would be ridiculous.

Noticing the drift in time she decided to get dinner going. She had made a great loaf of bread, so she decided to make pasta to go with it. She was rolling out the pasta dough when the back door opened, finally revealing Jorah.

"Sorry I was in there all day," they said as they appeared. "I'm having some issues with a client. I hope you weren't..." Their words trailed off as they took stock of the kitchen.

She looked around and realized she had cooked enough for a small army. She winced. "Sorry, I guess I made a bit too much. I'm used to feeding a lot of people in a day."

They shifted their eyes to her. She expected them to be angry, but instead, they smiled. "This looks amazing."

She smiled but said nothing. She was used to praise for her cooking, but coming from them, it felt different, more special almost.

"Maybe I can take some of this to the mainland with me when I go. I'm sure the crew working at the job site would love some."

She nodded enthusiastically. "Oh, please do. Be sure to ask if there's anything they like so I can make it next time." Maybe they would like something she'd never tried before.

Jorah came around the counter and stood next to her. "What are you doing now?"

"Chicken parmesan for dinner. I made bread, so I thought we could make garlic bread with it. I just need to make the sauce and finish up the pasta."

They nodded. "How can I help?"

They wanted to help? "Oh, it's fine. I got it. You relax. You've been working all day."

Jorah shook their head and stayed standing. "I'm sure you are capable, but I want to help. From the look of it, you've also been working all day."

Why? She swallowed her question. "Okay. Why don't you chop the vegetables?" She slid the cutting board and pile of already-washed vegetables toward them. They grabbed the knife, but she immediately stopped them. "Like this." She showed them how to hold the knife and how to properly chop. Her hands tingled at their contact, but she ignored it, focusing on her task.

They learned quickly, chopping quickly and efficiently. She showed them how to cut the pasta dough, and before she knew it, dinner was done. "Would you like to eat outside?" they asked once everything was plated.

When she nodded, Jorah grabbed a blanket, and they made their way out through the sunroom toward the beach. The sand was warm between her toes, and the warm breeze felt like a warm hug. They were a few feet from the water when they opened the blanket and spread it out. Even though they had arms, they used the top two tentacles as well, one holding their food and the other helping to spread out the rest of the blanket. It must be convenient to essentially have an extra set of hands.

They looked at her, and she realized she was staring again. "Okay, fine, I was thinking about how it must be nice to essentially have an extra set of hands. No judging though."

Fuck. She hadn't meant to say any of that. She expected them to take offense, but instead, they laughed. "I will admit, it's nice. I couldn't imagine only having two hands. I have no idea how you get anything done."

She glared at them, but could feel the smile pulling at her lips. "I get things done fine, thank you very much."

They laughed again as they dug in. Quinn watched as Jorah took a bite, worried they wouldn't like it, as she mentally picked out all her simple errors.

Her fears dissipated, though, when they again moaned around their bite and went straight for another. "I can't believe I helped make this," they commented after a while. "There's no way I would have been able to do this alone, not even with a detailed recipe."

"I'm sure it would have turned out just fine," she said. "You seem perfectly capable of following instructions."

They hummed. "Capable, maybe, but I tend to go off script. I'm much better at giving directions than taking them." Their gaze heated, and she felt her core flame.

She turned back to the ocean, needing to put some mental distance between them. It was obvious they would never look at her that way. She was here to repay a life debt, nothing more.

"So, do you have family on the main island?" she asked, trying to change the subject.

Their face fell a bit as they answered. "Not conventionally. I have a friend, Reka, whose family has kind of taken me in, but krakens are generally nomadic and don't spend much time together."

She frowned. "That seems lonely."

"I agree. I've always been the outcast of my kind because of that, but that's why I moved to Damona. I wanted more of a community, a homebase. Even though I'm the only kraken there, I'm not treated much differently."

She turned that information over in her mind. It must be hard to be so different from everyone around you. "That must be hard, but sometimes, found family is the best kind."

They cleared their throat. "Do you have anyone... missing you now?"

She winced at that. "Probably not. I had a few friends at school, but I was in the foster care system for most of my life, and I didn't really stay in contact with anyone after I started school."

"I see."

She quickly changed the subject, ready to talk about anything else. They discussed more casual things, like their favorite TV shows and lighter memories. She was surprised to learn that even though the island was generally cut off from humans, they still had access to social media and were caught up on current events. Soon, the food was gone, and they were just chatting about nothing. It all felt weirdly normal. They soon got up and stood in the water. It was warm as the waves lapped at her ankles.

"How fast can you swim?" she asked as they stood there, admiring the horizon.

"Very. The main island is a couple hundred miles away, and I can clear it in around ten minutes."

She practically snorted. "Wow, that's impressive. I never learned to swim."

"You can't swim?" they asked in what sounded like disbelief.

"Well, we aren't all born to swim," she said defensively.

"But no. I don't know how to swim." She looked at her feet in the water, visible through the crystal-clear water. She was glad she didn't fear the water after her fall. Looking at the ocean from the window had concerned her, but now that she was standing in it, there was no fear.

"I can teach you," they said.

She shook her head. "It's okay. You don't have to."

"I know," they said, "but I want to. Plus, what fun is living on an island if you can't enjoy it?"

She smiled tentatively. "I would like that, then. Thanks."

Once the sun started to set, they made their way back inside. Jorah allowed her to help clean this time, since they both cooked, but not without a bit of arguing. If she was being truthful, she enjoyed the light bickering they were developing; it was almost comfortable.

Once the night wound down, she wasn't sure what to do. She thought about joining Jorah where they sat on the couch, but she didn't want to overstep. Yes, they had been spending time together, but she didn't know what all that meant yet.

"I'm going to bed," she proclaimed way too loudly and way too awkwardly. Before they could even respond, she shuffled up the stairs and shut and locked her door behind her.

She flopped down onto the large, comfy bed, and sighed. Why did Jorah give her these butterflies? Why was she so nervous? Why hadn't they mentioned the life debt? There had to be something she should do to repay it and be on her way. She crawled up the bed, deciding to just sleep. She should shower, or at least change, but she didn't want to. Crawling under the blankets, she let sleep claim her, ignoring thoughts of Jorah and their kind smile.

12

JORAH

The next few days flew by, and they had developed an interesting rhythm. They woke up at the crack of dawn every day, courtesy of Quinn. She seemed to have a natural alarm that couldn't be broken. They would share breakfast, and then Jorah would work. They spent their days in their office. Not only did they think Quinn would appreciate the space, but they needed it as well. While a part of them wanted to spend all their time around her, sometimes, when they didn't spend enough time alone, they could get agitated, and they didn't want to snap at her. Ever. Work was a great excuse to be alone for a while.

After telling her how many people were on the crew, Quinn seemed to go a bit overboard. There was an abundance of pastas, breads, stir-frys, and pastries. Every day, there would be even more. The fridge was getting full, and they had a very large fridge.

Then, the two would cook dinner together. Quinn ran a tight ship in the kitchen. She was all about proper technique and was very particular about knife cuts, but she was also playful and an excellent teacher. Sometimes, they ate at the kitchen island, but most nights, they ate out by the ocean, talking about nothing and everything. They learned so much about their fated one in that time.

Jorah wished they didn't have to leave her today, but Kingsley was extremely demanding. The building wasn't even finished yet, but he was very concerned about aesthetics. That's why they're going in today; Kingsley claimed he needed to see the project in person to get the true vision.

Quinn seemed to have gotten up even earlier than normal and packed up all the food in the water safe containers Jorah had bought for this trip. As soon as the two were done eating breakfast, she came around and handed them another smaller box.

"This one is lunch for you. I noticed you haven't been eating lunch, so I made something you could take. It's just a sandwich and some fruit, so you can eat it quickly."

They looked at the box in their hands. To her, it might have been just a sandwich, but they'd never had someone who noticed things like that. At least, no one other than Reka. Guilt settled in their chest, knowing she was obviously thinking about them while they hid away in their office.

"Thank you, *mi sirenita*," they said, the endearment slipping out naturally. "I know I won't be here for most of the day, but you should try to relax. You've been working hard. It would be good to take it easy."

She looked at them like they spoke a different language.

"It would be good for you to relax," they continue. "Take it like a mini-vacation of sorts."

She snorted. "You want me to treat a kidnapping as a vacation?"

They shrugged. "Give it a try."

By lunch, everyone was tired and annoyed. The project was behind schedule, which meant investors were pressuring everyone to work faster. I set out the spread of food, hoping to brighten their spirits.

Workers started filing in, and the food went quickly, as expected. After eating, everyone seemed to be in a much better mood.

"Damn Jor," Triton, the head contractor said. "I didn't know you were a chef, too." Triton was a mage who they'd worked with on numerous projects.

Jorah smiled, pride filling them. "As much as I would like to, I can't take credit. I have a...friend who made all of this."

"Well, tell them we say thank you. It's been a lot with the higher ups on our asses, so this really hit the spot."

He nodded and turned to the crew, informing them it was time to work again. When everyone left in a chorus of groans, Jorah sat and ate their own lunch. The sandwich was perfect, as was everything else Quinn made. They soon saw Kingsley come around the corner and look at all the food.

"Wow, who brought all of this?" he asked, grabbing a plate and filling it with food.

"I did," they said. "I have a friend who made way too much food and wanted me to bring it in."

Kingsley let out a pleased groan, a sound Jorah had come to associate with Quinn's cooking. "This is amazing. Whoever your friend is has some real talent."

They smiled, pleased their fated one was getting so many compliments. "She does. I will let her know you liked it."

They finished their sandwich and went back to the crew with a smile that no bad, exhausting day could erase. Their fated one was brilliant, and they would do anything they could to keep her.

13

QUINN

Quinn tried to relax during the day, she really did. However, after reading for an hour in the sunroom, she couldn't do it anymore. She didn't want to do a ton of cooking again. Even though her fingers itched to be busy, she felt bad messing up the kitchen every day, and she didn't want to use up all the food.

She hoped those working with Jorah enjoyed her food. Even though she loved cooking, the real joy came from other people enjoying her hard work. More than anything, though, she hoped that Jorah liked their sandwich. It was simple, but she thought they may not want something that took time to eat. They seemed busy, and she just wanted to ensure they were eating.

This morning, she'd watched them take off their robe before going into the ocean, putting more of their gorgeous body on display. She knew she should look away, but it felt as if her eyes were glued to them. They obviously didn't care about being seen nude, so she didn't want to make a big deal out of it. However, she couldn't help but notice they didn't have any...anything. It looked like they were fully smooth all over, and she couldn't help letting her thoughts drift to all the possibilities that left.

To keep herself busy, Quinn decided to do some cleaning. While the villa wasn't truly dirty, she swept all of the sand outside, started the laundry, and washed all the windows in the sunroom. She also organized the living room and reorganized the kitchen. She still wasn't sure what the life debt entailed; she'd wanted to ask many times but ultimately decided against it. She trusted Jorah, strangely enough, but still worried she would anger them.

As she was folding the laundry, she heard the glass door slide open, turning to see Jorah stepping through. Water ran down their frame, and she had the wild thought to lick it from their chest.

What was wrong with her?

When they saw her, their face instantly lit up, sending butterflies straight to her stomach.

"Hello, *mi sirenita*. How was your day? Did you relax?"

She looked away to hide her blush. She still didn't know what that phrase meant, but they called her it an awful lot. "It was fine. How was yours?"

"Work was a bit nuts, but everyone loved your food."

"Really?" she asked, turning back to them.

"Really," they said with what sounded like glee. "There was none left. Everyone on the crew made it a point to tell me how good it was, including the guy in charge, and I loved my sandwich. It was just as amazing as everything else you've made."

She blushed again, which was something she'd been doing much more often. "Thank you. I'm glad you liked it."

They peered around the room then, suspicion falling in their gaze. "Did you clean in here?" they asked.

"Just a bit," she responded casually.

"How much is a bit?"

She shrugged. "Well, most of the house, but relaxing is boring."

They huffed. "That's it. I'm off tomorrow, and I'm showing you how to relax."

She was stunned, her mouth dropping open. "What?"

"Tomorrow, we're spending the day relaxing. I happen to be an expert on the topic."

She huffed. "What? Is relaxing part of the life debt?"

Amusement shimmered in their gaze. "It could be. I guess you'll find out."

Quinn woke with a start. She'd dreamt of tentacles surrounding her, making her feel safe and wanted. Soon, the touch changed to something much more sensual. They wrapped around her, tweaking her nipples and rubbing between her thighs. She felt them get tighter, turning her entire body into a livewire of sensation. She felt lips working their way up her neck, toward her chin. They were about to meet her own before her internal alarm clock slammed her out of her dreams.

She felt too worked up to face Jorah now. It must be because she really didn't have any alone time on the ship, plus her roommate's book choices had been living rent free in her head since she met Jorah.

She definitely needed to take care of this before spending the day with him.

Moving her hand down her body, she rubbed light circles into her clit before she grabbed one nipple and twisted it tightly between her fingers. Soon, her dream drifted back to her, and she could almost feel the tentacles wrapping around her body. They rubbed her clit and roamed across her skin. She thrust a finger inside herself, wishing it was thicker. She knew their tentacles would touch her everywhere at once, bringing her pleasure she could only imagine. Adding another finger, she imagined it was a tentacle working in and out of her. She worked herself until her orgasm crashed over her, and she rolled into the pillow, hoping to cover the moan she couldn't stop.

She fell back and relaxed into the bed, breathing hard. She had gotten herself off plenty of times, but this felt more intense than normal. Pushing up to her knees, she started to panic slightly. What were these feelings? Maybe it was just idle curiosity, but that's not what it felt like. It felt like more, *much* more. How could she be feeling this way? Yes, Jorah saved her, but they also kidnapped her. To her chagrin, even though she'd just got off, she craved more. She craved *them*.

She ran to the bathroom and turned on the shower to freezing cold, trying to tamp down the heat still radiating from her core. After she reined in her hormones, she got dressed in one of the new outfits Jorah had brought home and went to the kitchen. She'd planned to make a simple french toast this morning until she realized she already heard clicking coming from the kitchen. Quinn worried there was an intruder in the kitchen. Jorah was never up first.

To her great surprise, she found Jorah facing away from her, stirring what smelled like peppers on the stove. They'd put on her apron, which was way too small but made them look even more attractive than they already were.

After this morning's elicit thoughts, she felt like she was going to turn into a puddle on the floor. Before she could, however, Jorah turned to face her full on. "Morning," they smiled. "I thought I could make breakfast this morning."

While she liked the routine of getting up and cooking, Jorah *did* look good in the apron. "Is this a part of my relaxing day?" she asked as she jumped up on the bar stool. They were wide and backless to accommodate tentacles, but she didn't mind it. She actually appreciated how large all the furniture was in this house. Being fat, it was sometimes a concern that her body may not fit comfortably on furniture, but she never had to worry about that there.

She watched as Jorah added eggs to the pan and seasoned them. She saw the omelet break as they flipped it, but she couldn't care less. No one had cooked for her in a long time, and she felt like she was getting royal treatment.

They removed the eggs from the pan and buttered the toast when it popped. Soon, there was a plate in front of her–a pepper and mushroom omelet and toast. "This looks great, thank you."

They came around and ate with her. "So, what does a day of relaxation consist of for you?" she asked after a while.

Jorah smirked. "It's a surprise."

"Of course, it is." She rolled her eyes but felt a smile spread along her face. They finished their breakfast, and Quinn tried to come around to clean, but like normal, Jorah lifted her and moved down the hall.

"Put me down," she yelled, but they just laughed, ignoring her. No one had ever been strong enough to just lift her before. She knew she was heavy, but this feeling of care was something she could get used to, which scared her. They dropped her down into their bed, and she giggled.

"I have something for you," they said, moving to the drawer and pulling something out.

He handed it to her, and she realized it was a bikini and a see-through wrap. "What's this?"

"I know humans typically wear special clothing to swim, so I bought this for you."

It was deep red with gold detailing along the clasps, the coverup matched flawlessly. It looked like one of those expensive bathing suits you would see in one of those 'most expensive bathing suit hauls' on YouTube.

"I figured you could wear it and we could try swimming. If not, we can at least stand in the ocean."

She nodded. "Thank you, Jorah. This is really nice."

He smiled softly. "I like getting you gifts. If you want, you can change in my bathroom, and we can go down."

"Okay." That admission stopped her in her tracks, but she didn't want to think of that now. She moved to their bathroom and closed the door, staring at the suit in her hands. Quinn wasn't usually so self-conscious. She had learned a long time ago that some people despised fat bodies just for existing, and that was their problem, not hers. However, she *was* a bit nervous about Jorah's reaction. She looked at it again but made the decision to wear it anyway. If Jorah had a bad reaction, that was on them, not her.

She put on the suit and cover. Even with the coverup, she could still see the stretch marks around her belly and a bit of cellulite on her thighs and ass, but she decided she wasn't going to care.

When she emerged, all her nerves instantly dissipated. Jorah's gaze was so heated, she thought she might catch on fire. She left the coverup untied, and she watched as their gaze roamed over every inch of her exposed skin. It felt like a caress, smooth and sensual, and she felt herself getting wet on the spot.

She cleared her throat. "So, should we go?"

They blinked out of their daze. "Uh, yeah. I'm ready."

The weather was perfect today. A warm breeze blew past as they padded down to the ocean, and the waves crashed against the shore in a soothing rhythm.

Jorah brought out a large blanket. She could feel their eyes on her still, and from behind, she could assume what they were staring at as they settled on the beach near the water.

"I know I already said it, but it's so cool you basically have another set of hands. I wouldn't have been able to do that on my own."

They looked at their tentacles. "I will say, they're pretty useful. Makes it easy to multi-task." She thought about some of the multitasking she'd dreamt about and felt her face get hot. Thank goddess it was hot; she could use that as an excuse.

Jorah started going through their bag and pulled out a bottle of sunscreen. "I know humans are sensitive to the sun, so I thought this would help."

"Thanks," she said as she reached over and grabbed it. Even the sunscreen looked luxurious. "Where did you get this? I mean, I appreciate it, but isn't everyone who lives on the island immune to the tropical weather?"

"Not really. It's a place for all supernaturals, not just ones who primarily live in the ocean. Some people even have vacation homes on Damona, but they live with humans most other times.

"I see. It's fancy," she mentioned.

"I guess. I like nice things."

She snorted. "I could tell."

"What's that supposed to mean?" they asked. Their words sounded accusatory, but they lacked any bite.

"You're just kind of a snob. I mean, I'm sure even your toilet paper has a high thread count." She paused and her eyes widened. *Fuck.* She hadn't meant to say all that, and she hoped it didn't hurt their feelings.

When she looked up, all her fears subsided. Jorah was laughing, their smile wider than she'd ever seen. "That may be a fair assessment. I like to think I'm classy."

"Right," she giggled as she smeared on the sunscreen. She caught Jorah watching and apparently, the sun was already getting to her, because she began moving slower, rubbing the lotion up and down her legs. She moved up to her midsection and higher, adding more and rubbing over the top of her cleavage. She had ignored them up until this point, but she peeked over to see them following her touch with an intense gaze. They weren't even trying to hide it. Once she was done, she held the bottle out to them. "Would you do my back?"

"Of course." Their voice sounded hoarse and needy, matching the way she felt. She spread herself out on the blanket and heard the bottle squirt before she felt their hands on her shoulders. The sunscreen was warm, like they'd rubbed it between their hands to heat it up. They worked thoroughly, rubbing the lotion in hard, as if it were a massage instead.

Soon, she felt two tentacles rubbing down her arms as their hands moved down her back. Memories of her morning came flooding back, and she squeezed her thighs together to try and get some friction. Instantly, her nerves made her still as she focused on ignoring the heat building in her lower belly.

They worked their way down her back, getting close to

her backside, but they skipped over it and moved lower. If she was honest with herself, she was a bit disappointed, but was also glad they respected boundaries. They moved down to her calves, working their way up. They moved to her thighs, starting on the outside but slowly moving inward. The touch turned into more of a caress, their tentacles following close behind their hands. She imagined them moving higher, grazing her clit and bringing her to climax.

When she opened her eyes, she realized the touch was gone. She sat up, her face on fire. Jorah's gaze didn't leave her, but they didn't make a motion to move. They were almost unnaturally still.

They cleared their throat. "Should we get started?"

She nodded, not trusting her voice. They helped her to her feet, never releasing her hand as they strode to the water's edge. The water was warm on her feet, and she was thankful for it as they waded in until she was waist deep. Jorah gave her some pointers before they started, but they were born to swim. It was as natural as breathing for them. The whole time, they made her feel safe and secure, even though she worried about drowning every three seconds.

Quinn wasn't sure how much time had gone by, but soon, her muscles were sore, and she was getting tired. She'd managed to float pretty well, and she'd even done some successful doggy paddling. As if Jorah could tell she was getting exhausted, they mentioned going to shore.

When they reached the beach, Jorah told her to stay put and scurried inside. She wrapped herself up in her towel and sat on the blanket. Even though she was soaking wet, the breeze was so nice, she was comfortable.

Soon, Jorah returned with a basket. "What's that?" Quinn asked as she wrung out her hair.

"Lunch," they shrugged. They joined her on the blanket and opened the basket to reveal two bento boxes.

Quinn smiled. "Thank you. I could have made lunch."

"I was glad to do it. I don't suspect it will be as good as what you can do, but I thought it was okay."

"I bet it will be great." She opened the container to find pasta with vegetables in it and mango on the side. "Oh! I love pasta salad," she exclaimed. She quickly grabbed her fork and dug in. It was tangy and delicious, the dressing tasting handmade. "This is amazing."

Jorah's face turned a deeper blue that she hadn't been expecting. "I'm glad you think so. I looked up a recipe online after you mentioned you had a fondness for it."

"You remembered that?" She had mentioned it in passing once, nights ago. She'd told them about a barbecue hosted by her group home when she was young. Everyone had chipped in, but the woman who ran the house, Marty, had asked her to make the pasta salad. She had no idea what that was, but she'd been given a bunch of ingredients and made it work.

That night, just about everyone had complimented her on her pasta salad. They said it was the best they'd ever had, and it was the only dish completely gone. She had never been told she was good at anything before, and that feeling drove her forward.

"Of course I remember," they said with a smile. What was she going to do with this kraken? They made her want things, want *them*, more than she'd ever wanted anyone. "So, can I ask how you ended up in the ocean?" they asked carefully.

The change in subject made her whip her gaze toward them again. Anger welled in her chest thinking about it. "I was pushed," she said simply.

They gasped as their face turned hard, their expression as angry as she felt. "By who?" they asked quietly.

She looked at her hands. "A prick named Brandon Cotley. His father is a super famous chef, which was the only reason he got the internship in the first place. He was mad because I was getting all the praise and he wasn't. He was drunk and we fought. He kept pushing me toward the edge, and I tried to push him away, but," she sighed, a tear falling from her eye, "I just fell backward."

They nodded, digesting the information. "If you wanted me to, I could take him to the bottom of the ocean." Their words were so serious, and while they should have scared her, they made her feel protected and safe instead.

She had to look away. Her face was on fire, and she couldn't contain the butterflies that felt like they would burst from her chest, alleviating some of her anger. They leaned in to wipe away one of her tears, and, finally allowing herself to look into their eyes, she saw a fierceness there that sent an inferno loose in her lower belly. It felt as if time had stopped around them. Even the sound of the ocean seemed a distant memory.

They were sitting close. Even though Jorah was much taller and sat differently because of their tentacles, it was like the two had gravitated together.

She leaned in, or they did, she wasn't sure, and they were only a breath away. "Can I?" they whispered.

"Yes."

Their lips collided, and it felt magical. She had been kissed before, but it never felt like this. Jorah deepened the kiss, taking control. Suddenly, she felt tentacles circle around her waist and lift her toward them. She squealed in surprise, but it was quickly covered by Jorah's mouth. They supported her bottom, and she wrapped her legs around their middle. Their hands gripped her hair, their nails scraping her scalp. She was suddenly acutely aware that there was only a scrap of a bathing suit between them, and even that felt like too much.

Soon, she felt them reach for the ties on the bathing suit, but before they came undone, Jorah pulled back and looked her in the eyes, assuring what they were doing was okay. She bit her lip and nodded, and they didn't need to be told twice. The bottoms and top were gone in a flash, and finally, she was completely bare in front of them.

It was like her dream had come to life. Their tentacles were everywhere, tweaking her nipples and wrapping around her inner thighs. They weren't slimy, but smooth, making her body feel like it was on fire. Their mouth moved down her neck as they nibbled the sensitive spot between her neck and shoulder.

"Jorah, please," she panted.

"Please what, *sirenita*?"

"I need more."

They didn't disappoint. "Lay back," they murmured as they lowered her to the blanket and continued their exploration down her body. They moved slowly, as if worshipping her body. Using their tentacles, they parted her legs. She felt exposed and wanted to shift away, but soon, she heard a rumble of delight from Jorah's chest.

Their fingers moved to her cunt and spread her wide. She could feel how wet she was, and she turned beet red as they dragged a finger through her pussy and brought it to their face. They licked her wetness from their digits, then closed their eyes and hummed.

"You taste divine. Tell me how to please you."

She blinked, trying to turn her brain on. "What?"

"I am not experienced with humans. How do I pleasure you?"

She could feel her face catch fire. She'd never had to explain sex to someone before. "Here," she gestured to her clit. "It feels good when you rub here." Before she could blink, they dove in, bringing their tongue to her clit. They moved it around, testing her reactions. From there, they took control, moving with expert skill.

They sucked and tugged on her clit, moving their tentacles to keep her thighs spread wide. Two of them worked up her middle, plucking her breasts. She had never experienced this much stimulation at once. Using their fingers, they plunged two inside her, reaching for that sensitive spot she knew would have her seeing stars.

Quinn reached down and grabbed the two tendrils near the top of their head. They groaned as she did, sending vibrations straight to her core. She squeezed them tighter, pulling another moan from them. The sound was intoxicating, and the only one she could hear over her beating heart.

"Fuck, Jorah, I'm gonna..." The words barely left her mouth before they picked up their pace, and she was pushed off the edge.

They kept up until it was too much, and Quinn was pushing them away. They released her, but quickly readjusted her to lay against their chest. She laid there contentedly, happy for their cool skin against her flushed body as Jorah kissed her shoulder and settled behind her.

The sun set as they laid there, Jorah rubbing their arms and tentacles up and down her body, as if they couldn't get enough. "What does '*mi sirenita*' mean?" she asked. "You call me it all the time."

"It means 'my little mermaid,'" they replied simply, without any more explanation.

She laughed at the implication, but also felt warmth bloom in her chest.

As the sun set and the stars lit above them, the air became cool. "Would you like to go inside?" they asked.

When she nodded, the two packed everything up and headed inside. Once they moved, it was like the bubble had broken, and she didn't know where to go from there.

"I should...I mean...I'm going to shower." She scurried away, not wanting to make them uncomfortable, but a tentacle wrapped around her arm before she could. It wasn't a tight hold, but enough to make her pause. This casual touching had become a norm she was enjoying.

When she looked at them, they looked surprised at their own actions. "Would you like to shower together?"

Her body shivered in delight. "I would like that. Very much."

14

JORAH

Jorah walked Quinn toward their room with excitement lodged deep in their chest. They hadn't expected her to be interested in them this way. Yes, they had touched more casually as of late, but they hadn't wanted to make assumptions, hadn't wanted to hope too much. But when they had seen her in that bikini, it took all their strength to not fuck her into the bed right then. When they were in the store and saw that maroon shade the day before, they knew it would look perfect on her.

They had been more than right.

Then, when they saw the heat in her eyes, they knew she felt it. The connection. Maybe not as strong, but it was there. And the way she *tasted*. There had never been anything so sweet.

Now, they were dragging her into their room, their shower. She insisted on putting her swimsuit back on back at the beach, even though they informed her no one would disturb them. When they climbed into the shower, she turned to them, looking timid once again. Jorah realized quickly she liked praise and reassurance, which they were happy to provide.

"May I?" they asked, placing their hands on her waist where the ties sat.

She nodded shyly, and they pulled the strings, letting them fall down her legs. She turned and allowed them to untie the back ones as well. They appreciated the generous swell of her ass and thighs–they wanted nothing more than to be back between them. She faced them and let the top fall.

They admired her, drinking her in from her pussy, which they were sure was still wet, to her breasts, which they wanted to fill their hands with.

Turning, they managed to drag their gaze away and get the shower started. They hadn't even thought to ask what temperature she liked, but she seemed relaxed as they stepped in, so they assumed they picked the right one.

They picked up the soap and held it up. "Can I wash you?"

She once again nodded, and Jorah worked the shampoo they bought for her through their hands and to her hair. The eucalyptus and mint scent filled the shower as they worked their hands through her soft strands, massaging her head as they went. Soon, she let out a moan, and they suddenly needed to pull as many from her as they could.

Once her hair was rinsed, she took the soap away and squeezed it on her hands. "Is there..." she started but stopped for a moment. "I don't mean this to sound insensitive, but is there anywhere I should worry about getting soap? I assume not your gills, but anywhere else?"

They smiled at that, pleased she would take such consideration. "Just my gills, *mi sirenita*. Everywhere else is fine."

She nodded and got to work. Her smooth hands slid

across their skin, leaving a warmth wherever they traveled. She started at their chest, moving gently down their arms. Her gaze was scrutinizing–not in a judgmental way, but like she wanted to learn their body. They knew they were cooler to the touch, but their skin also felt different. It bounced a bit like silicone, but with a softer feel. She soon moved lower to their tentacles and grasped the first one at the base, slowly working her way up.

"Hm," she said to herself.

"What?" they asked.

"What?" she parroted.

"You hummed."

She quickly turned a violent red. "Oh. I mean, I was just thinking how most animals with tentacles have suckers."

They almost laughed. "Ah. Yes. No suckers here. It's a good thing, too. On land, I'm sure I would stick to everything."

She giggled at that and continued her perusal. "That's true. I know you said you don't speak to your parents much, but did you grow up on land?"

They swallowed, thinking about their family. "No. Most krakens remain in the ocean."

"But you didn't?"

"No. My parents wanted me to, but I refused. Krakens are rather antisocial, as many ocean dwelling beings are. Even when they couple, they stay long enough to raise the younglings into adolescence, and then it's a sort of fend for yourself situation. We are territorial by nature, so keeping others at a distance is considered normal."

"That sounds lonely."

"I thought so too. That's why I left. I was always different. I didn't want to be territorial or alone. I met Reka, and she introduced me to the island. She grew up there, and nymphs are very collective. I got really into art and design, and her dad helped me secure an apprenticeship in Spain. That's what I've been doing ever since."

She considered their words. "Wait, how did you work in Spain? I think someone would have noticed a kraken walking around."

They smiled. "I used a magic talisman to disguise myself. I could have remained in the human lands forever if I wanted, but I prefer being free in my skin. Plus, I'm essentially the only designer on the island, so I'm always in demand."

"I see. Can you bend? I can't quite reach," she said, motioning to their head. They complied, bending so she could wash their head. It reminded them of when she gripped their tendrils when they were between those soft thighs. They weren't aware how sensitive that area was, but when she gripped it again, they almost groaned.

"I think it's nice you found Reka," she said as she washed and rinsed them. "Not everyone fits into the mold they were born in, and it's okay to be different."

Her words settled deeply within them. They knew what she said was true, as their therapist had said similar things for years, but hearing it come from their mate felt different. They let out a hoarse laugh. "Though I don't enjoy being alone all the time, I'm still stubborn, and I sometimes worry I'm designed to be alone. As if one day, I'll push everyone too hard, and they won't want me around anymore."

She readjusted and looked them right in their eyes. They had no idea why they said it, but that was the truth. It felt like those deep brown eyes were looking straight through to their soul. They stared back but held their breath, waiting for the rejection, for the agreement.

"I don't think so," she said simply.

"How could you know?"

"I know we haven't known each other for long, but I can tell. Though you're stubborn, you're thoughtful and obviously care for those around you. I'm here to repay a debt, yet you bought me an ice cream maker."

They huffed. "That was just to con you into making me ice cream."

"Whatever it was," she continued, "you were thinking about me. I can tell you do that for others. People won't leave you, not because you buy them things, but because you care."

Their throat felt dry. Even though the shower was running, they could only hear the beat of their heart, or maybe it was hers. They leaned in, and without a second thought, kissed her hard. She kissed them back, wrapping her arms around their neck. They were a mess of teeth and tongues, and they wrapped their tentacles around her, needing to be closer. Their hands dug into the swell of her ass and bent her knees, lifting her in the process. She squealed, and they greedily swallowed the sound. Using another tentacle, they shut off the water then carried her out of the shower. Having multiple limbs had always made multi-tasking easier, and it was truly paying off now.

They moved her to the bed, laying her in the middle and slanting over her body. "Wait," she said. They paused immediately. "I don't want to get the bed all wet."

They grinned. "*Mi sirenita*, it's fine. I can just change the sheets later."

"If you're sure."

Jorah answered by kissing her again. She bit their bottom lip, and they groaned. They felt their cock protruding, and felt almost embarrassed, but there was no way to stop it. They continued down, kissing across her jaw and down her neck.

She ground against them, and when she pushed against their cock, they almost came. They moved to her breasts, taking one in their mouth as they wrapped the other in a tentacle, flicking the bud until it hardened. She wiggled under their touch, moaning their name. Hearing it come from her mouth soothed them, and they wanted, no, *needed*, more.

They used two tentacles to spread her knees and open her legs wide. With another, they slithered up her thigh and plunged into her. She gasped at the sudden intrusion but started moving with them. They pulled back, watching her writhe beneath them. They couldn't look away. They felt the squeeze of her inner walls around their tentacle, and imagined what it would feel like around their cock. They continued working in and out of her in a slow rhythm. They reached a bit further, and she jolted, crying out.

"Yes. There, please," she cried. Jorah repeated the movement, feeling for the place that made her moan. Once they found it again, they didn't let up. Every time they thrust in and out, they purposely put pressure on that spot, using another tentacle to rub the small nub above her opening.

"Yes, Quinn. Come undone for me." Within seconds, they felt her walls tighten as liquid rushed around their tentacles, their gaze moving to her face as they watched her fully unravel.

15

QUINN

Quinn laid there, trying to bring her soul back to her body. She had never experienced that much stimulus at once, and it was overwhelming in the best way. As she came to, she noticed Jorah was still looking at her, almost with reverence.

She suddenly noticed their tentacle was still inside her when they wiggled it again. She gasped, and they continued, moving slowly but purposefully. "Jorah, please." She wasn't even sure what she was asking for.

"What, *mi sirenita*? What do you want?"

"I..." What did she want? For them to stop? Keep going? Her brain was too scrambled to put together a full thought.

They continued their slow, agonizing pace, rubbing against her G-spot with every swipe. "I know what you want. You want me to bring you pleasure again, don't you? You want to be a begging mess beneath me. Want me to care for you and decide when you get pleasure."

She did want that. How they knew all that, she didn't know, but she nodded anyway.

They continued moving in and out of her, using their hand to rub her clit. "I want to give you more. Can I?"

She wasn't even sure what that meant, but nodded anyway, trusting them completely. Soon, she felt another slickened tendril snaking its way up her inner thigh. She knew what they were planning, and she tensed instinctively, having never done anything like this. "Relax for me, *sirenita*. I've got you."

Quinn trusted them. She didn't know why, but she did. She felt that tentacle snake up higher, pushing in to join the other. Taking a deep breath, she forced herself to relax. After some work, the second tentacle had slipped in, and she was unbelievably full.

"Ah, fuck," she moaned.

"My sweet, you're so soft, so tight. You take my tentacles so well. I can't wait to sheath my cock in this tight heat." Their dirty talk was something she didn't expect, but it made everything hotter. "You're doing such a good job for me. You're such a good girl."

They held her hands above her head and cradled her entire body in tentacles. It was a comforting sensation, only adding to the pleasure. "I'm going to come Jorah," she breathed.

"Yes. Come for me." Their words were her undoing. She came so hard, she saw stars. It was like an out of body experience she never wanted to come back down from.

When she did, however, reality came rushing back to her. Jorah had wrapped her up once again and laid next to her, but this time, she felt claustrophobic.

"Um. I'm tired. I think I'm going to go to bed."

Disappointment momentarily flashed in their eyes, but they only nodded and released her. She crossed her arms, suddenly feeling a bit shy. She could feel their gaze on her the entire way to the door, but she was too nervous to look back at them. If she did, she might have done something foolish.

Like stay.

Once she was back to the safety of her room, she crawled into bed and wiggled under the covers, ignoring the regret she felt about not sticking around. She had never come that hard or that many times in a row...ever, not even on her own. It all felt confusing, and she thought about it long into the night.

Maybe this is what they needed. Maybe the life debt was companionship. Maybe they were just lonely and decided a human would be fun for a while, but for how long? How long would it be until they bored of her? From human myths, it seemed like mythical beings tended to live long lives, sometimes forever. Was she just a passing phase? One human of many?

The thought made her heart feel like lead, and she had no idea why. Just because they had been intimate didn't mean they owed her anything. She was no one's toy, no one's side project. She wasn't one of many.

It took her a while, but she finally drifted off, trying not to think about what the future held.

16

JORAH

The next week went by in a new routine, and Jorah wasn't complaining. Every morning started the same: Quinn making breakfast and the two of them sharing a meal. Then, they went to work, and she cooked all day long. When they were back on the mainland, they bought her some cookbooks, and she dove right in. Before long, she had them spread out with sticky notes and highlighters everywhere, like she was studying for an exam.

Then, at night, they would have their normal dinner, and Jorah always helped. Once everything was cleaned, they would take her to the bedroom and bring her all the pleasure they could before she would sneak off to her own room. They wanted to ask her to stay, but they didn't want to push her too far too fast.

Over the past couple days, however, Quinn had hinted at...more. They knew they had no chance of hiding their cock, not when her beautiful body was on display. She'd made it obvious she wanted to pleasure them, but they were worried. They knew they didn't look like a human, and their cock was certainly different. They worried that she would see them and be disgusted. They didn't know if they could handle that kind of rejection.

"Jorah, are you coming?" They heard her call from the kitchen. Looking at the clock, they realized it was getting rather late, so they closed their laptop and put everything away. They were sure the hotel job would be the death of them. Kingsley wanted to open before the summer came, to capitalize on the island's biggest travel season. But between the delays with getting permits and his intervention down to the last sheet fiber, it wasn't looking great.

None of that mattered right now, though. Work was over, and what mattered was their beautiful Quinn downstairs, cooking without them. They worked their way down the hall and froze when they saw her. Bent over the oven. With nothing on but her apron and a thong. The view reminded them of the painting Reka had made, but the thought fled as they gazed at her.

She stood up and pulled a dish out of the oven. Though it smelled amazing, they couldn't give a shit what it was. When she turned, her gaze landed right on theirs. The apron was maroon, which they had learned was her favorite color, with white lace accents on the edges. They saw it when making a run to the chef supply store and couldn't resist, and they were so glad they'd picked it up.

Her breasts poured out the sides, and her wide hips reached outside the fabric, making them want to grab on and never let go. Her cheeks were flushed, and they weren't sure if it was from having her head in the oven, or because she was standing basically naked in front of them.

It took them a while to actually speak. It felt like they were standing there forever, but for no time at all, either. "You look..." they couldn't even finish the sentence. They rushed her instead, taking the pan from her hands and shoving her up onto the counter in one swoop.

"Oh my god, are you okay? That pan was piping hot."

She reached for their tentacle, but they weren't concerned. They barely felt it. They slid their hands up her thighs, trailing them under her apron. "What's all this for?" they asked.

"What do you mean?" she responded, putting on her best doe eyes. Jorah noticed she pretended to be coy often, and it was a game they were more than willing to play.

They worked their way up her chest, sliding the apron over to tweak her nipples. She gasped, leaning into their touch. "Why are you out here, naked and ready for me?"

"I just wanted to surprise you," she breathed.

"Well, I'm certainly surprised." They wrapped around her, ready to have their way with her right there on the counter.

They pushed her back and she went willingly, resting her ass on the marble. They reached below and pulled on the thong with one swift movement, ripping it clean off.

She gasped, but they swallowed it with their kiss. She wrapped around them, her pussy flush against my body. Grinding against me, she searched for friction, that I wasn't ready to give.

"Please," she said against their lips.

They wanted to tease her as they sometimes did, but they couldn't, they were too wound up. Their tentacles went straight to her ankles, pushing them apart, looking like the best meal they could ever ask for. They started at her ankle, kissing down her calf, worshiping her beautiful body. Soon they reached her thighs, and was almost at her pussy, when she stopped them.

"Wait," she said, and they froze. "Let's go to bed."

They nodded and moved her to the bedroom. She was wrapped around them, mouthing their neck, sending shivers down their spine.

When they dropped her to the bed, her apron pushed to the side, showing off her luscious curves. They could feel themselves hardening, but moved over her so she wouldn't see. They slanted their lips over hers for a kiss as her hands began roaming down their arms and across their chest. Suddenly, they started roaming lower. They didn't think anything of it, until they felt her shimmy down a bit, obviously with a goal in mind.

A bit panicked, they grabbed her hands with their tentacles and shot them up, holding them above her head. "What are you doing, *mi sirenita*?"

Her face flushed. "I -- we've only been focusing on me. I thought tonight, we could focus on you."

Oh no. They didn't know if they could handle rejection right now. Not tonight. "But I love focusing on you, and you seem to enjoy it too."

"Yes, but I want more."

They quirked a brow. "More?"

She moved to sit up, and they released her arms easily. "Yes, Jorah, more. I like what we've done, but I feel like you're hiding from me. If that's it, if this is some part of the life debt or whatever, I don't want that." They blinked at her, processing her words as she continued. "Whatever. Just forget it."

Quinn made to move, but Jorah caught her before she could get far. "You and these damn tentacles," she mumbled under her breath, though she made no effort to move from their hold.

"This has nothing to do with the debt. I'm just...different from what you might be used to. I don't want you to be disgusted." They averted their eyes, not wanting to see her reaction.

She laughed, shocking them. When they looked into her eyes, they expected to see hesitation or sympathy in her gaze, but neither were present. It looked more like amusement. "Jorah, you're a kraken. I would say none of this is 'what I'm used to'," she said with air quotes. "I honestly think it would be stranger if you had a human dick."

They couldn't help it–they laughed at that, too.

"So can we just...try?"

They thought for a moment, taking what she said into consideration. "Fine. But if you're not into it, just tell me. We can go back." They weren't sure if that was true, but they had to hold on to hope.

She nodded, her expression never wavering as she pushed them back until they were lying on their back. They stared at the ceiling, still worried about her reaction. After their conversation, their cock had tucked back in, but they hesitantly released it.

She gasped slightly, but they tried not to react. "Is there anything you don't like?" she asked.

They pulled their gaze down, making eye contact with her, worried about what they'd find. There was no fear or disgust in her eyes, which made them release a breath they didn't know they were holding.

"No."

17

QUINN

Jorah wasn't kidding when they said they were different. She had figured it was internal, when she'd seen them naked many times over. However, she was no less surprised by what she saw. Their cock was the same color as their body, but it turned a more navy blue at the tip, the head larger with a thicker rim. It looked as if a small tentacle was snaked down around it, and it was bigger than any she'd seen before. The thought of what that may do inside of her had her lower belly heating to an almost scorching temperature. They didn't have balls, but a lower hole where she assumed their cock tucked in.

After determining they didn't have any dislikes, she wrapped her hand around them. Even though they were stock still, she could hear their breath catch as she began moving her hand up and down. They were already lubricated, her hand gliding easily across their shaft.

She doubled her efforts until a small drop of pre-cum dripped from the tip. Leaning forward, she licked the droplet up with the tip of her tongue. Jorah wrapped their tentacles around her head at her touch–not in a forceful way, but in a grounding movement. It gave her the courage to continue, taking them further into her mouth. They moaned, finally relaxing a bit underneath her as she continued her exploration, sucking them as far as she could go before having to come up for air, then moving her lips down the side, her tongue gliding across the tentacle there.

"Fuck, *mi sirenita*," they gasped, "just like that. You make me feel so good." She flushed under the praise before she brought her hand to the base of their cock, experimentally touching the opening below. Feeling them tense once more, she immediately stopped. She started pulling her hand back, but they caught it with their tentacle. She looked up at them, waiting for some direction.

"You can..." they started, "I've just never..."

"It's fine. I was just curious."

Jorah must have seen something in her eyes, because they shook their head. "It's okay. I want you to."

She nodded but moved her hand back to their shaft to angle their cock to her lips. They relaxed again, hissing as she lightly scraped her teeth along the underside. Her hand snaked down once more, moving toward their hole. She teased the area slightly, circling her fingers around the entrance.

After a few minutes, Jorah interjected, "You're killing me. Please, I need more."

Having them writhing underneath her with pleasure filled her with a deep contentment she wasn't interested in evaluating too closely right at that moment. She did as they requested, plunging her fingers in their tight heat. They moaned loudly, gripping her hair harder. She moved her fingers and continued sucking, loving the sounds they made, the sounds she drew out of them.

"I'm close," they said in obvious warning, but she didn't waver. She increased her pace, taking them even deeper. Once they hit the back of her throat, she swallowed around them, and that was their undoing. She felt hot liquid hit the back of her throat as they came, and she did her best to swallow. There was more than she was used to, and it ended up running down her face.

Once they finished, she was up in the air, being carried again like she weighed nothing, repositioned to hover above them. Without warning, they licked her from ass to clit, and she had to catch herself from falling, balancing until they pulled her down over them.

"Wait," she gasped.

That caught their attention, and they stopped. "What's wrong?"

"I'm just too heavy to sit all the way down."

Quinn felt their breath rush across her clit as they huffed, causing her to shiver. "*Sirenita*, I would be one weak kraken if something like that could hurt me. Don't worry about me. Relax and take your pleasure."

She still wasn't sure, but their words relaxed her enough that they pulled her right down. Their tongue snaked inside her, and she felt them sliding it in and out, fucking her slowly. She started grinding down onto their face, all her worries gone as she became lost in the pleasure they gave. She came with a scream, all but falling to their chest.

When they finally pulled away, she had to take a deep breath. "I want to be inside you, *sirenita*. Can I?"

She nodded. "Do you have condoms?"

They thought about it. "I don't, but I can't spread disease, and kraken mating is...complicated. In simple terms, I can't get you pregnant unless I actually try to."

That was definitely something she wanted to learn

about later, but she was pretty single-minded at the moment. "Then yes."

"Tell me you want it. I need to hear it."

The word need stuck in her head. "I need you to fuck me, Jorah, please." The words were barely out of her mouth when she was flipped so she was straddling their waist. Their still very hard cock pressed against her ass, and she rocked back against it before they lifted her up and adjusted her over them. She worked herself down, stretching over their large length.

"Fuck." They were definitely bigger than any human she'd been with, bigger than any of her toys. The stretch felt like a bit much, but once she was used to it, it hit all the best spots, causing pleasure to build once again. She wanted them to move, but she knew they were waiting for her to adjust. "Jorah, please," she breathed, not able to articulate herself properly.

"Please what, *sirenita*?" they asked with a smirk on their face.

While she wished she could find something snarky to say in that moment, she couldn't concentrate on anything else. "Move. I need you to move."

Their smirk dropped, and they wrapped their tentacles around her as they started moving. Instead of thrusting from beneath her, they tightened their grip slightly and moved her body. It made her feel more like an object than a person, and it turned her on more than she could express. It made her feel used in the best way. She could feel that extra snaking tentacle rubbing against her G-spot, and it took all she had in her not to explode then and there.

"You feel so tight wrapped around me," they moaned. "Like this cunt was made for me, made to bring me pleasure. I want you to come all over my cock. I'm not gonna last."

One of their tentacles moved to her clit, adding the extra push needed to send her over the edge. Her vision whited out for a moment as pleasure coursed through her body. She had never experienced something so intense. When she came back to reality, Jorah was losing their rhythm and after a few thrusts, they stuttered beneath her as they finished. She could feel the warmth pool in her lower belly as their cum filled her past what she thought was possible.

Quinn fell back, unable to hold herself up, but Jorah caught her before she could go tumbling off the bed. They gathered her into their chest and readjusted until they were righted by the headboard. They rubbed her back in soothing circles, causing her eyes to close.

"That was..." she started.

"Yeah," Jorah said, squeezing her tighter. The moonlight seeped in through the curtains, bathing the room in light.

Quinn shifted uncomfortably, not sure what was expected of her now. She knew she instigated this, but did Jorah want her to go? Were they just being nice because she was a fragile human? "Um, I can go back to my room if you'd like."

They stared at her like she'd grown a second head. "Is that what you want?"

She knew she should say yes. "No," she said instead. "I just wasn't sure what you wanted."

"Oh, *mi sirenita*, I want you here. Always."

The words sent butterflies exploding through her stomach. She should go back to her room and stop whatever they started. There was no way it would end well. She was being kept against her will, and if she was ever given the opportunity, she would go back.

Right?

That wasn't something she needed to worry about now, though. For once, she wanted to be a bit selfish and let future Quinn deal with the consequences.

"Okay. I'll stay."

Quinn woke to the sun filtering in through the curtains and tentacles surrounding her. She made to move, but quickly realized she was trapped in a tangle of limbs or... tentacles. She maneuvered around until she was face to face with Jorah, their blue skin glowing in the soft morning light. It was early, but she was always an early riser. It was obvious Jorah was not. They usually woke a few hours after her, and never said anything before they had a cup of coffee.

She looked at them for a while. They were so relaxed in their sleep. Even though they normally carried themselves with a carefree attitude, there were stress lines that were missing while they slept. Their constant worry for those around them and how they felt was a constant weight on Jorah's shoulders, she could tell. It was unnecessary–it was impossible not to like them.

Even if they'd kidnapped you.

Deciding it was time to get up and start breakfast, she tried to break free of the sea of tentacles. Her attempts seemed in vain, though, as she would move one, and another would tighten. She huffed in annoyance. When she was almost free, she felt arms come around her middle and pull her flush against their body.

"Where are you going?" they asked sleepily.

"To make breakfast, like I always do."

"No," they whined. "It's early. Stay in bed with me." They nuzzled into her neck, drifting back off.

If someone were to tell her a week ago that this giant blue kraken was a cuddler, she would have laughed in their face. She rubbed her hands over their head, and they sank further against her.

"Come on," she said after a few minutes, wiggling once more. "I need to use the bathroom, and you told me you had to go to the job site today." She had made a bunch of Indian food the day before for them to bring in. There were curries, samosas, biryani, and a bunch of naan that she actually needed to pack before they left.

They kissed her neck briefly before releasing her. "Fine, but only because you need to go to the bathroom."

She laughed. "If I didn't, you would what? Keep me here forever?"

They smirked. "Don't threaten me with a good time."

The butterflies started up once again. She hustled to the bathroom, then to the kitchen to make breakfast and pack everything up. She noticed the lasagna pan still sitting there uneaten from the night before and flushed, thinking about the distraction she'd caused. She wasn't sure what had gotten into her, but she didn't regret it.

Soon, Jorah sat down and ate with her. Then, they were out the door and in the water. It was sort of strange to watch someone go to work through the ocean.

Either way, she decided she would actually try to relax today. After making naan by hand and being fucked into oblivion yesterday, her body was tired. She went to the living room, grabbed a book off the shelf, put on one of the swimsuits Jorah got her, and went outside.

The sand was white and soft, softer than the sand she felt in Hawaii. Thinking back to her first visit to the beach, she couldn't believe it was only a few weeks ago. It felt like a lifetime ago. While she had loved working on the boat and going to school, she couldn't deny that it was nice to have some down time. She had been going for so long, and while she still enjoyed being busy and having work to do, Jorah showed her the importance of rest and having fun.

What did it all mean? They were only keeping her there for a life debt. Maybe they were lonely? They seemed to have friends and people around, but maybe they wanted companionship. Maybe that's why she was there. While she enjoyed her time with Jorah, she didn't want to start a relationship on the foundation of kidnapping.

Relationship?

The thought stopped her in her tracks. Did she want a relationship with them? The word yes rang in her ears way too clearly, but that would be ridiculous. She should want to go back to her life, but did she? Really? She for sure didn't want to be kept as a pet, but it didn't feel like that. The more she thought about it, the more she warmed to the thought of staying here. What would she do? She had to work; she would become antsy if she didn't.

Her thoughts were interrupted by a break in the water. She'd assumed Jorah came back until she realized it wasn't them. This person had long white hair and icy blue skin. She looked to have normal legs and hands at first glance, but they were webbed.

Quinn stood and looked around for a weapon. She wasn't sure how much damage she could do, but she wasn't just going to let this creature do...whatever. She found a piece of driftwood next to her and held it up in a way she hoped was intimidating.

"Who are you?" she called as they approached the shore.

They paused, holding their hands out like they were trying not to spook a cat in an alley as opposed to talking with another person. "Hello. I am Solise. I do not mean you any harm, human. I am just here to speak with Jorah. I am a family friend."

Quinn squinted at her, trying to tell if she was telling the truth.

"If the name Reka sounds familiar, that is my daughter. I am her mother."

She stared for a moment longer and dropped her piece of wood. Jorah *had* mentioned they were basically family. "Oh. Sorry. Jorah told me no one could come here."

She nodded. "I understand why you might think that. It is not warded from anyone they deem trustworthy. You are Quinn, correct?"

She blinked at that. Had Jorah talked about her? "I am."

Her eyes softened in a way akin to a proud mother. "I'm glad you are here, Quinn. May I come inside? I have something to discuss with Jorah."

"Oh, they aren't here. Jorah had to go to the main island today."

Mischief twinkled in her eyes. "They told you about the mainland?"

Shit. Maybe she wasn't supposed to say that. "Yeah. It's a paranormal paradise," she joked, trying to lighten the mood. "The true Area 51."

She laughed. "I guess you could call it that. Could I come in anyway? It has been a very long time since I've spoken with a human."

"Sure," she shrugged. Pulling her wrap around her tightly, she made her way inside, Solise following close behind. They moved into the kitchen, where Solise sat at the kitchen island, looking comfortable. "Can I get you anything? We have tea, and I can whip something up quickly if you're hungry."

"I would accept some tea if you have it, but that's all. Though I have heard you are an excellent chef."

"You have?" she asked, surprised.

"Oh yes. I know some of those working on the new hotel, and every time Jorah comes with food they talk about it for the rest of the week," she laughed to herself.

Quinn flushed at the compliment. "I'm glad they liked it."

"Yes, well, I would suspect nothing less from Jorah's fated one. They deserve someone like you."

Quinn blinked. *A fated what?* "I'm sorry? A fated one?"

Her eyes widened for a fraction of a second before she schooled her features. "It seems they haven't spoken to you yet. I assumed they had, since they asked Reka for my help."

Quinn continued staring, hoping for more, but it looked like she wasn't going to share further. When Quinn didn't speak, Solise tsked.

"I would like to tell you more, but it isn't my place. I'm sure you and Jorah will have much to speak about." She stood, obviously planning to take her leave. "Whatever they tell you, I suggest you have an open mind. It might sound like a lot, but the fates are never wrong. If you could, let Jorah know I have the answers they were searching for." With that, she took her leave, leaving Quinn shell-shocked at the kitchen counter. Maybe Quinn should have stopped her or made her explain what she meant, but she could tell she wouldn't get her to break that easily.

What was a fated one? Was that why she was here? She moved to the couch and bundled up, trying to wrap her head around everything. One thing she knew for sure was that Jorah had a lot of explaining to do.

18

JORAH

Jorah reached the mainland beach with time to spare. Though the containers of food slowed them a bit, it was nothing too difficult. Since they were early, they decided to stop by the Ocean's Cup, a coffee shop they used to go to every day before work. They hadn't been in the past few weeks, too eager to get the job done and get back to their mate.

Today, though, after they'd been together, there was a new lightness to their soul. They knew they needed to tell her about the fated pairing soon. They didn't like lying to her, and they especially didn't like her thinking she was there over some life debt. It was time, and while they couldn't be sure she would instantly accept them, they hoped she would want to try. It would be complicated, but maybe they could take her back and live under the guise of being human. It wasn't their favorite option, but they would do anything for her.

The bell above the door chimed as they entered the coffee shop, greeted by the rich scent of coffee and the sound of milk steaming.

As they stood in line, a voice called them from behind. "Long time, no see, stranger," Reka said as she walked up to them.

They nodded in greeting. "Hey Re, how is everything?"

"Can't complain. What are you doing here? I thought you were honeymooning it up with your fated one?"

They sighed. "I was, but Kingsley insisted I be on site for every step of the process, even though I can't do anything until there's walls."

Reka laughed, but then her eyes widened suddenly. "Wait! You're here today. Mom was going over to talk to you this morning. She has news from the council."

Jorah felt all the air leave their lungs. Not only were they worried Solise would scare Quinn, but if she mentioned her being their fated one, it could ruin everything.

"Can you deliver these to the worksite?" they asked Reka. "I need to get back."

"Yeah of course, but you owe me. I'm still taking care of your plants," Reka smirked.

"I know, you're my savior. Once this is all done, come for dinner. Quinn loves to feed people, and her cooking is exceptional."

Reka laughed a nod. "Fine, and I want one of your alocasias. The one in the living room. I've grown attached to it."

"Deal." They handed over the boxes and raced out of the cafe, back to the water.

They made it back in record time, moving up the beach and through the sliding glass doors faster than they'd ever gone. They looked around frantically, only to find Quinn burrito-ed on the couch in a blanket.

"You're home," she called, but her voice was barely over a whisper.

"I am." They sat on the edge of the couch. "So, I heard Solise stopped by."

"She did. We had a nice chat."

Her clipped tone didn't make Jorah feel confident about her not knowing. "So, I'm assuming she mentioned fated ones?"

She shrugged. "It came up."

That didn't bode well. "And what did she say?"

"Not much. She wanted you to tell me. The whole conversation hinted at you lying to me, though." She shifted up, looking directly at them, waiting for an explanation.

Her words hit them square in the chest. "I guess I should start at the beginning. Before we met, I could...feel you, your soul. My attunement to the ocean told me I needed to go to you. I didn't know it was you at the time, but I started swimming until I felt you again. By then, you had been pushed off the boat, so I picked you up and brought you here."

Her gaze never wavered. "What does that have to do with us being fated whatevers?"

They sighed. "In my world, a fated one is the person who completes you, someone perfect for you in every way. Some think it's an evolutionary trait, while others think it's a blessing from whatever otherworldly entity they believe in. I didn't even think krakens had them, due to our independent nature, but as soon as I found you, I just...knew."

Her eyes softened for a moment before hardening once more. "Why didn't you tell me?"

They looked down, unable to meet her eyes. "Like I said, I didn't even think krakens could have mates. For a while, I thought I was fooling myself, hoping for something that wasn't actually happening. Once I knew it was real, I was worried you would reject me outright. I mean," they wiggled their tentacles in demonstration, "I'm not exactly what you're used to. Plus, I'm not even sure if I could be a good fated one. I am much different from my kind, but I'm still stubborn and selfish, and I like being alone sometimes. I don't really think I deserve you.

"I am so sorry for lying to you. The life debt was a lie. There are only stories of krakens who would save humans to incur a life debt, but no one has done that in a very long time. I just needed an excuse for you to stay here. I thought if I could keep you here for a little while, I could sway you. Obviously, that was wrong of me, but I can't even say I wouldn't do it again."

At her gasp, they elaborated. "If it gave me this time I've had with you, I would do it one hundred times over, because this has been the best few weeks of my life. I know that makes me selfish, but it's true."

They continued staring out the glass window, sure her silence was rejection. They thought about bolting, getting as far away as possible. They knew rejection was a strong possibility, but they had let themselves hope, for just a moment, she wouldn't. Unfortunately, not only were they too different, but they had lied to her. "I can take you back. It will be hard, but I'm sure we can..."

Jorah's words were interrupted by Quinn grabbing their chin and turning them toward her, and the tears in her eyes nearly broke them. "Quinn, I'm sorry. I never meant to lie to you. I just wanted you close. Please don't cry, I can't stand it."

"I'm not crying because you lied to me, you silly kraken." She giggled at her own words but continued. "I'm crying because even though you were wrong, that is the sweetest thing anyone has ever said to me. Maybe you are a little selfish and a little stubborn, but I'm not perfect either. While I don't like that you lied to me and will probably need some time to trust you fully again, I can't deny that I feel...I don't know. I feel for you more than I have in a very long time. I don't want this to end."

Jorah could feel tears falling from the corners of their eyes. "Do you mean that?"

She shifted closer, and they couldn't help it–they gathered her up until she was sitting in their lap. She giggled slightly as they shifted but sobered once they were settled. "I do," she finally said. "I don't know how it'll work. I love my job, and I want to keep doing it."

They caressed her face. "We can do anything you want, *mi sirenita*. We can go back, and you can finish school. I'm not sure if I can get your internship reinstated, but I will do whatever I can, if that's what you wish."

"But what about your business? You can't just leave."

They shrugged. "I have enough money to support us for a while. I could always design in the human world. I just want to be wherever you want to be."

Tears rolled harder down her face at their words, but they just wiped them away for her. "Why are you crying now?" they teased.

She poked them in their side hard but with a smile. "I'm just...glad I found you, regardless of circumstance."

Their smile grew. "I am too."

Taking a deep breath, Quinn rested her head against their chest. "So, what now? Do you have to go back to work?"

They sighed. "I probably should, but I'm not going anywhere."

She grinned, sitting up to look at them. "We could swim again."

"I would love nothing more."

19

QUINN

Quinn woke with a smile on her face. After they worked on swimming yesterday, they had lunch and spent the rest of the day on the couch, watching movies. Well, watching was a relative term. They spent a little bit of time watching, but a lot more time trading orgasms.

Those romance books weren't too far off the mark. Tentacles were truly a gift.

She quickly realized she was no longer drowning in a sea of tentacles. Bolting up, she noticed the bed was empty. When she looked outside, she guessed it must be a bit later than she normally woke, but nowhere near late enough for Jorah.

Even though she had her own clothes, she threw on one of Jorah's massive robes and made her way out. She heard laughter coming from the kitchen that was distinctly not Jorah's. When she got there, she saw Jorah, Solise, and someone who she assumed to be Reka sitting around the kitchen island. Jorah's gaze immediately honed in on her, like they sensed she was present. Reka noticed their gaze and turned to see her.

"You're awake!" she shouted, jumping down from a stool and running to her. Quinn's eyes widened when Reka embraced her, but she hugged her back, feeling a strange mix of awkward and happy.

Reka was tall and slender, her skin the same blue as her mother, her hands and feet webbed, her hair brown and cropped short. She had a button nose and freckles.

"I've been waiting very patiently to meet you. I wanted to see you the minute Jorah found you, but they said you needed space to adjust." She narrowed her eyes at Jorah, and they rolled their eyes, still holding their smile. "Anyway, you're gorgeous. Everything I thought you would be."

She flushed under the compliment. "Thank you. Jorah has told me so much about you. They've shown me a bunch of your art."

"All good, I hope. I'll make you anything you want once we get back to the mainland. I know you'll want to do some redecorating. We can totally shop for whatever you want, on Jorah's card, of course."

Quinn blinked, stuck on Reka's previous statement. "Mainland?" she asked.

"Yes," Solise spoke up this time. "My daughter is skipping a few steps," she said with a glare in Reka's direction, though it held no real heat. "I came to speak with Jorah because when they found you, they had asked me to speak with the island counsel regarding your extreme circumstances. Normally, humans aren't allowed on the mainland, but the counsel has made a[l] n exception as their fated one."

She nodded, slowly digesting that information. "So, I can go to the mainland?"

Solise nodded. "Yes, but you must complete the bond first. The counsel will only allow it if the bond is completed, after which you will be given an amulet showing your exception, though I don't think you will have any trouble. Most on the island are very open, and they all love Jorah," she said with a wink in their direction.

Jorah's cheeks darkened. "I wouldn't say that," they muttered under their breath.

"Nonsense!" She pinched their cheek like they were a child. "Everyone loves this face." Quinn and Reka had to muffle their laughter as Jorah tried to squirm away.

Solise turned serious once again. "There's no rush. Bonds are considered sacred, unbreakable once they are solidified." Solise seemed to sense her slight panic, because she quickly amended, "I don't say this to scare you. I only want the best for you both. While I do believe the fates are never wrong, I want you to make an informed decision."

She only nodded, still trying to digest.

"Well, when you two are ready, let me know and I will get everything settled. Come, Reka, let's let them have breakfast."

Reka pouted, still holding Quinn around the shoulders, but she pulled away and looked at her. "Once this is all settled, you and I are going to have the best time." She leaned in and whispered, "plus, I have all the best, embarrassing stories on Jorah."

"You know I can hear you, right?" Jorah called from the kitchen.

Before Solise stepped out of the door, she turned back to a laughing Quinn. "One more thing. This is a personal request, but I would love for the two of you to have an official ceremony, the way humans do when they are married. It doesn't have to be soon, but I would love to see

Jorah have one." She smiled at them, and then she was gone.

A small smile graced Jorah's face as they moved behind Quinn to kiss her neck. Her body shivered at the contact, and she melted against them.

"Your family is nice," she breathed.

They took in a loud breath. "Yeah. Sometimes it's hard to think of them as family, since it's not something I'm well acquainted with, but I love them like family."

She smiled. "When you've found your people, that's all that matters."

"Oh, I've definitely found my people," they said as they lifted her.

She squealed as they moved her around to set her on the counter, bringing them eye to eye. "I am never going to get used to you doing that."

"You should. I plan on doing it for a very, very long time." She stiffened at their comment, thinking about the bonding Solise spoke about.

"What is a bonding?" she asks them hesitantly.

"A bonding is where two fated souls tether. Every species has a different process, but it will make it so that if one of us leaves this Earth, so will the other. There could be other side effects, though. I don't know anyone else mated to a human, but you may pick up some of my abilities."

Her eyes widened. "Like what?"

"I couldn't tell you for sure. I know you won't become full kraken, but I know you will live much longer. Even for a kraken, I'm young, with many years left. You will be more immune to disease and injury."

Protectiveness flashed in their eyes, making her stomach heat. "How old are you?"

"I'm not exactly sure, but I believe I'm only a hundred and fifty-three, give or take."

Quinn blanched, and she struggled to form words. "I'm sorry...you're a hundred and fifty?"

They nodded. "A kraken's life span is normally around six hundred or so, but I've known some to live longer."

She gulped. "I could live to five hundred?"

"Give or take. *Mi sirenita*, I know it's a lot to take in. There's no rush. While I want to bond with you more than anything, I would never force it upon you. However, I promise if we do, you will want for nothing. It would be my pleasure to take care of you for as long as we live."

She felt her sinuses swell and tears fill her eyes. How was it that this kraken made her cry at every step? She never cried. They gently cleared her tears as she hugged them, and they fell into her embrace.

She wasn't sure if this was smart, or if Stockholm Syndrome or whatever else had settled in, but the idea of having Jorah by her side forever filled her with a sense of joy she never wanted to lose.

"Let's do it," she whispered in their ear.

"What?" they asked, pulling back and looking into her eyes.

"I want to complete our bond. This might sound ridiculous, but something inside of me knows I want to be with you for the rest of my life. There's no reason to prolong it. We can work out the rest on the way."

Their shocked face morphed into a smile that melted her heart. "My fated one, my goddess, I would be honored to complete our bond."

She nodded, throwing them an equally as large smile. "So, what do we do?" They lifted her once more, carrying her outside. "Where are we going?" she asked.

They didn't answer, setting her down on the sand next to the water. "Do you trust me?" they asked.

"Yes," she whispered without hesitation.

"We need to get in the water. The bond starts there. We're going to go underwater, but I promise, nothing will happen to you."

She looked at the water and nodded. While she was getting the hang of swimming, she wasn't sure how long she could hold her breath.

They helped her get undressed before pausing to look at her face. "Are you sure Quinn? This means forever."

She nodded instantly, so sure of her choice. "I want you in my forever."

Their gaze softened as they nodded. "Okay." They picked her up and carried her into the water until they were almost under. "Ready?" they asked.

She nodded and held her breath. They sank them under, and all the sound from above was quickly replaced with the almost-silence of the water. Her eyes were closed, but she could feel their lips on hers, trying to deepen the kiss, but she panicked for a moment, worried about opening her mouth underwater.

"I've got you," she heard before she melted against Jorah. When she opened her lips, it almost felt like an air bubble entered her mouth and trailed down to her lungs.

In a panic, she gasped, but her mouth didn't fill with water as she expected it would. Instead, she gasped normally. She squealed in surprise, and they laughed. "I can breathe underwater!" she exclaimed.

"Yes. I noticed. Is anything else different?" they asked.

She looked around. She could hear more sounds now, like the water didn't muffle her ears, and she could open her eyes without the salty water burning them. She could see them perfectly now. Underwater, their skin was shiny, and they looked in their element as they gathered her up and kissed her deeply.

While she wasn't paying attention, they lifted them both out of the water and back to the shore. "Where are we going now?" she asked, pulling away from the kiss.

"Somewhere I can ravage you properly," they growled.

She snorted. "Naughty kraken."

"For you? Always."

They carried her through the house to their bedroom, and once they'd made it to the bed, she reached her hands up, feeling the expanse of their chest. Caressing her chin, they leaned in, kissing her. This was a different kiss than any of the ones they'd shared previously. While it was rough and needy, it was also intense and passionate. She couldn't stop. They deepened the kiss, and she went pliant under them, happy to let them lead. Their hands rubbed up her thighs, wrapping around to her ass and giving it a tight squeeze. They snaked their tentacles up her middle, wrapping them around her breasts and plucking her nipples with the tips.

"Oh fuck," she sighed into their mouth. Their kisses moved down her neck, to the spot where her shoulder and neck met.

"*Mi sirenita*. You're so beautiful. Not a thing in the world compares, especially while I'm buried deep inside you." Their hands shifted back up to her knees, and they all but folded her in half.

They used one tentacle to run through her pussy. "And you're already so wet for me. I love it." Their tentacle plunged inside of her at the same time their tongue met her clit. She cried out, fucking herself on them, trying to bring herself release. Their touch was always intense, but this felt different, like *more*.

They continued licking and sucking, soon moving their tentacle out of her, and she whimpered at the loss. She felt one hit her back entrance, and she gasped. "Is this okay?" they asked.

She nodded, wanting to feel everything with them. They seemed to want to change angles, because they lifted her, and soon, she was turned around, her face next to their cock and her ass in their face. She felt like she should be self-conscious, but she wasn't. It was almost like she could feel their want for her in the air. She stroked their cock a few times before taking the thick head into her mouth, licking up all the pre-cum pouring out.

Jorah leaned in and licked all the way from her clit to her ass. They stayed there, tonguing her hole like someone who hadn't eaten in days. She'd never had anyone do that to her, and while it was odd, it only heightened her pleasure.

"Yes, Jorah, please. That feels so good." She swallowed them back down, wanting to pleasure them just as much as they pleasured her. She reached down for their lower hole and fingered it with one, then two fingers. She found that sensitive spot inside and rubbed against it, causing them to buck into her mouth.

All too soon, she was flipped back onto the bed with them hovering above her, sinking into her quickly. She wrapped around them, her nails digging into their back as they thrust in and out, keeping a steady pace that drove her even closer to the edge. Soon, she felt a tentacle teasing her other hole, and she leaned into it, craving the full feeling she knew she would get. She wanted to be consumed by Jorah. They worked the tentacle in slowly, moving in short thrusts until they were fully seated.

"Oh fuck, I'm so full," she gasped out.

"You feel so good wrapped around me. I want to be here forever." They continued their rhythm, never letting up.

"Jorah, I'm so close. Please let me come."

Instead of teasing her like they normally did, they increased their speed, hitting all the right places until she fell apart beneath them with a scream. They continued until they lost their rhythm and came deep inside her.

They flopped down on top of her, crushing her beneath them. Suddenly, it was like she felt a click in her soul, and she could feel a flow of love that wasn't coming from her. She gasped, poking Jorah until they moved to the side and looked at her. "Do you feel that?"

They nodded, staring dreamily at her. "I feel you right here," they said, pointing to their chest.

"I feel..." She wanted to say loved, but she didn't want to put words in their mouth.

"If you feel what I'm feeling, you should be feeling the love I have for you."

"What?"

"I love you, Quinn. You've been my universe from the moment I met you, and you will be for the rest of my days."

She sharply inhaled and buried herself into their chest. "Ifeelthesame." She could hear how muffled she was, but they weren't letting it go.

They moved her so she was un-burrowed and faced her. "What was that, *sirenita*?"

"I feel the same. I know it's absurd and too fast, but I love you. So much."

"Everything is absurd with fate, but this is perfect."

She burrowed back in. It *was* perfect.

20

JORAH

The next few days were filled with sex, naps, and snacks, which was the ideal way to live, in Jorah's opinion. The bonding rut was strong, and they could barely let her out of their sight long enough to relieve herself. In fairness, she was equally as needy, never letting them get too far away.

After about a week, they felt ready to go to the mainland. As Jorah gathered the last of their things they wanted to take this trip, they saw Quinn staring wistfully at the room. They could feel her sadness and moved to wrap her in their arms. "What's wrong, *mi sirenita*?"

"Nothing," she said with a shrug. "I'm just a bit sad. I mean, we've spent all our time here, and now, I feel like we're abandoning it."

"Oh, my love. I know the feeling, but we still own this place. We can come back whenever we please. Just say the word, and we can be here."

She nodded, sinking deeper into their embrace. After a few moments, she turned. "The only human and the only kraken on the island. We will make quite the spectacle, don't you think?"

They laughed with a nod, loving how she made light of everything. They gathered her up and carried her to the beach. They would never tire of carrying her everywhere.

They swam her to the mainland, moving slowly so she didn't get sick. With her being able to breathe underwater, it was easy to travel with her, but speed was still an issue. They reached the beach quicker than they expected, and they set her down once they reached the shore.

Her eyes were wide, and they could feel her curiosity. The island looked a lot like other island nations, with large buildings spread across the skyline. "This is beautiful," she said in awe.

"Yes. I do love it quite a bit." They gripped her hand as they walked along the streets, and before long, they were at their townhome, light blue on the outside with a white roof.

They opened the deep purple front door into the living room to find it still covered in plants, minus the alocasia missing in the corner. Quinn walked around, taking it all in. Unlike the villa, this house was cohesive, with blue and white patterns and tiles in each room.

Even though they could feel her now, they waited patiently for her reaction. She turned to them and smiled. "Where's the kitchen?"

"Why am I not surprised?" they chuckled before leading the way. This home was open concept as well, but the kitchen was double the size. They never knew why they'd chosen a place with such a large kitchen, but now, it made sense.

She squealed and ran around like a youngling in a candy store when she saw it. She opened the empty fridge and gushed at the amount of space. When she turned back to them, she beamed. "This is perfect."

Once they got settled, Solise and Reka made an appearance, Solise formalizing Quinn's presence with the medallion before they stayed for dinner. They had graciously brought some groceries, and Quinn whipped up sushi like it wasn't that hard.

"This is the best piece of sushi I've ever put in my mouth!" Reka gushed as they ate.

Quinn flushed, and embarrassment flooded her as it always did when she received compliments. "Thank you, but it isn't anything too special."

Nonsense," Solise chimed in. "I've been around a long time, and this is special for sure."

The conversation flowed naturally, and Jorah could feel Quinn feeling accepted into their family. They wanted that for her so badly, and they were ecstatic it had happened.

Once they finally got Reka out the door, she wrapped herself around Quinn. "I'll be over tomorrow so we can go shopping. I know the best places. Plus, I can take you to get some more kitchen stuff."

"Sounds like a plan," Quinn smiled at her.

She then hugged Jorah, tugging his ear as she pulled back. "You be nice to her now, or I'll tell her all about the summer you got sunburnt."

Quinn giggled, and they smacked her hand out of the way. "You will do no such thing."

With a wink, she was gone, and Quinn shut the door before turning to them. "That was fun."

They huffed, still annoyed with Reka, but smiled anyway.

"Stop," she said, bumping into them. "You know you love her."

They huffed again but laughed this time. "Come, *mi sirenita*. Let's go shower."

"Together?" she asked.

"Of course."

The next day, Jorah was needed at the hotel site. Even though Kingsley had been understanding of their mating time, he wanted them there while the wallpaper was being installed to ensure it fit the vision. Quinn offered to come with them, excited to see them in action, and there was no way they could refuse. They stopped at the coffee shop on their way over, and the selkie woman behind the counter gave Quinn a free croissant, wishing their bonding well.

When they arrived at the sight, many of the crew members stared. They'd expected this, but they'd wanted to pluck all those staring eyes out so they could keep them off their love. Sensing their jealousy, Quinn wrapped her arm around theirs and kissed their shoulder, setting them at ease.

Throughout the day, many of the men stopped by to praise her food and thank her for it. When they were on their way out, Kingsley stopped them. "Jorah, I'm glad I caught you. Who is this?" he asked, looking at Quinn.

"My fated one, Quinn. Quinn, this is Kingsley. He's the one building this hotel."

She waved. "Nice to meet you."

Kingsley smiled. "Believe me, the pleasure is mine.

Quinn, I wanted to speak to you about something quickly. Could I steal you for a moment?"

She looked at Jorah, and while they wanted to say no, it was her choice. She turned back to Kingsley and nodded.

They stepped away, and Jorah waited impatiently. They weren't gone long, and Quinn seemed to be concealing her feelings, which made them nervous. What could Kingsley possibly need to speak with her about?

When she returned, her eyes were wide, but they didn't sense panic. She grabbed their arm and walked them out without saying a word. Once they emerged outside, they turned to her. "So, what did he say?"

She looked them in the eyes, and they could sense a lingering excitement beneath her hesitation. "He wanted me to run the hotel kitchen."

"What?"

"He said they hadn't found a head chef yet, and after he had some of my cooking, he knew it had to be me. I told him I had never run a kitchen and hadn't even finished culinary school, but he didn't care. He said the offer was there, and if I wanted it, the job was mine."

Pride beamed inside of them for their love. She was the only one who questioned whether she could do this. "It's up to you, love. I will say, I think you would do an excellent job, b. You would make them so much money, they wouldn't know what to do. But it's your choice. We have so much time to think about this, and we can do whatever you want."

"I love you too. Always."

EPILOGUE
QUINN

Quinn was chopping the last of the carrots, looking around her kitchen. She couldn't believe she was saying that: *her kitchen.*

A year ago, when Kingsley offered her this job, she couldn't fathom doing it. She was sure she would fail. With Jorah and Reka's encouragement, though, after falling in love with Damona, she accepted. She hired all her own staff and even got to build the menu. She spent months agonizing over every little detail, and opening day went off without a hitch.

A few months after she started, Reka showed her a news article about Brandon. Apparently, he'd tried to cover up what happened, but a camera on the ship caught it. Now, the only place he was cooking was prison, and she couldn't be more relieved. Though things didn't work out the way she thought they would, this felt better than anything she could have imagined.

Now, she was prepping for the most important day of her life. Lost in her thoughts, she didn't notice Jorah sneak up behind her until their tentacles wrapped around her.

"Don't you know you shouldn't touch someone with a knife in their hands?" she asked, trying to add a bite she didn't feel to her words.

"I'm not worried," they murmured. "I know how skilled you are with your hands."

She flushed and set her knife down. "What are you doing here?"

"I'm bringing you home. Everyone has it handled. You need to rest."

She looked around at everyone prepping for tomorrow. She knew and trusted her team, but she wanted it to be *perfect*. "Fine," she sighed, allowing Jorah to lead her out.

"See you tomorrow, Chef," her crew members shouted as she closed the door.

"Oh," she turned back, "Don't forget..." Before she could finish, Jorah lifted her over their shoulder and carried her out. "Hey!" she exclaimed. "I needed to say something really quick."

"It's never really quick, *mi sirenita*. I'm not letting you stay." She huffed but allowed them to carry her out. Some of the hostesses giggled at her predicament on the way out, but they were all used to it.

Once they were home, they settled her into bed and curled around her. "Are you ready?" they asked.

She nodded. "I'm nervous," she admitted. Even though they were mated, this still felt like a big deal.

"Me too, but I'm down for anything that allows me to show how much I love you."

She giggled. "I love you too."

The next morning, Quinn sat in their bedroom at the summer house, Reka flurrying around her with all sorts of makeup brushes and products. She was already in her emerald-green dress, her hair finished. Over the last year, Reka had truly become like a sister. Quinn had never formed any close relationships in any of the homes she lived in, and now that she had it, she didn't know how she'd gone so long without it.

"Okay," Reka said, setting the mascara down. "I'm done."

She turned Quinn to the mirror, and she gasped. Her long locks were half up, woven with different flowers. She wore a maroon dress with wildflowers snaking up the bottom. Her makeup was simple, highlighting her face in the best way. "You're a miracle worker."

"No. You're' just gorgeous and easy to work on," she chuckled with a smile. "Are you ready?"

She nodded. They slowly made their way to the beach, where the ceremony was being held. They decided that was the best place to have it, since that's where it all had started.

Reka went first, giving her a wink as she moved down the aisle. Soon, the music shifted, and it was Quinn's turn. She took a deep breath and turned the corner. The beach was lined with a white linen fabric all the way to the end. All their friends and family were there, smiles wide across their faces. Reka stood at the end as the officiant, waiting for her.

Then, there was Jorah.

They stood just in front of Reka, wearing a maroon, silk

robe. They had gold ringlets throughout the tendrils on their head and looked to have a bit of eyeliner on. They were stunning, and she could feel the love going both ways. Their breath audibly caught as they looked at her, and as she made her way down, she could see their eyes water. She had never felt so beautiful and loved in her entire life.

Jorah was right.

She would never want for anything ever again.

The End.

ACKNOWLEDGMENTS

Thank you to everyone who reads and loved Washed Up (With a Kraken). You are the reason I do this, so thank you. Also thank you to my partner, who supports me through my writing and listens to me talk about tentacle sex. Finally, thank you to my family for the support, and especially my mom, who always tells me to go back to writing, and stop procrastinating.

ALSO BY L.E. ELDRIDGE

Snowed Inn (With a Demon)

ABOUT THE AUTHOR

Lexie is a paranormal romance author and avid reader from Upstate New York. She runs an editing and PA company Morally Gray Author Services and lives with her partner Adi, dog Layla, and cat Swiper. When she's not reading (which is rarely) you can find Lexie playing video games or looking for amazing indie bookstores and vintage shops. Lexie writes campy books full of smut with simp-y monsters looking for love.

Lets Connect!

Printed in Great Britain
by Amazon